A Christmas Project

/

By

Wm. Sharpe

Edited by

James R. Sodon

Edited by James R. Sodon

Cover image by Elise Eggemeyer

ISBN: 9798583641833

Published 2020 by
BearhounD7 ProductionS LLC
Saint Louis, Missouri
BearhounD7ProductionS.com
Available from Amazon.com and other stores

Dedication

For my wife, Linda
For my daughter Sondra, I love you and miss you
For James R. Sodon, my friend, editor and conscience
For Eric Eggemeyer and Elise Eggemeyer, my "kids"
For Kenneth "The Neth" Harrison, my friend and favorite poet,
    cartoonist and composer, you are missed
For Drew Foster, my friend and a dreamer, you are missed

For Pam

How do you say goodbye to a friend, a gatekeeper, a confidant, a big sister, one who protected you from those who would do you harm and one who protected you from yourself at times? How do you say goodbye to someone who knew and understood, with almost a sixth sense, who was ethical and honest and who was not? How do you say goodbye to someone whose only flaw was that their sense of humor was similar to yours?

The answer is you don't. You feel the loss, you shed a tear because you will miss that they are not there, but you don't say goodbye. You say farewell and if you believe in something bigger than yourself, you say, "See you on the other side," and you smile, remembering your friend.

Thank you to

The Ladies of Edit Ink:
Wanda Sodon
Karen Eggemeyer
and
Linda Eggemeyer-Sharpe

Also
Baron, Ruby, Tink and Sheiky
our family's best friends
who always make me smile

Chapter 1

It was now mid-July, about nine months since Nick Caldwell put away those responsible for the deaths of his children. After searching for them several years and finally accomplishing that, he began evaluating cases, hoping to find one that he could immerse himself in.

Finally, he called his sister, Laura, and his brother-in-law Bob to ask a favor. He asked if they could loan Alex Papadakis, whom he had worked with on what's referred to as the *Not Forgotten* case, thanks to the writer who cannibalizes his cases and does not change the names enough to protect anyone, innocent or guilty. This writer has even suggested that Nick go on a book tour with him. Nick declined.

Alex Papadakis was a veteran detective in the St. Louis Police Department for forty-five years. He was a nice man, a gentleman and one of the best detectives Nick had ever worked with on a case. He reminded him of Sinclair Stewart, the New Orleans detective that Nick worked with all the time, but Alex wasn't a world champion smart ass like Sinclair. That is why Bob and Laura got the call instead of Sinclair.

He wanted Alex to mind the Clark Street office while he went on vacation. Alex agreed and moved up to Chicago. What Bob, Laura and Alex did not know was that Nick's vacation or staycation would last for the next four months. His business partner, Bart, didn't know that, nor did Nick's conscience, Mrs. Marbulls, or his wards Katie and Greg or his brothers Wil and Phil. In fact, Nick didn't know it either.

One day in early August, Nick just decided to stay home; he lied to himself and said he was going to take a sabbatical. After all, professors take them, so why shouldn't he. He called Bart and told him he would not draw his salary for a while, nor would he be coming into the office.

Nick's plan was simple: isolate himself from everything, grovel in self-pity, talk only to his dogs, Baron and Ruby, watch movies, read books and skulk around the city at night. He took down the calendars and put away all the clocks. He didn't plan to interact with anyone besides Baron and Ruby; they would be and remain his only company. He got rid of all the phones accept one, in case he needed to make a call to the vet for the dogs or 911 for himself. That's right, Nick Caldwell has gone around the bend because this is the only way he believes he can get through another holiday season alone.

He didn't get the closure or the relief he had hoped he would get by finding his children's killers. What was different? They were gone and he was alone. Nick wasn't suicidal; he didn't care that much.

Now a more rational version of Nick Caldwell, like the guy who cleared Tim McCarty's name or tracked down his wife who orchestrated McCarty's demise or the guy who solved a forty-year-old cold case or the guy who solved the murder of a retired Chicago wise guy's uncle, would never have considered doing what Nick Caldwell was doing. That Nick Caldwell might have embraced his family and friends and tried to work through the emptiness that he had felt for so many years after he lost his family. He would have kept busy with cases, rooting for the Bears, Cubs, and secretly for the Cardinals, Pirates and since the acquisition of Tom Brady the Tampa Bay Bucs. He would be complaining about the media, the state of Chicago, the country and the world.

This Nick Caldwell decided to take the "Oh woe is me tour." He did this because Nick had a secret; well, it really wasn't a secret. Everyone who knew or cared about Nick knew that he had a self-destructive streak as long as the Mississippi River and sometimes as wide as Lake Michigan.

The absent Maureen Richards, the woman who loves him and the one who for years was planning on murdering him (well, he did shoot her sister after all), she called it Nicky's death wish. She credited that for why they continued talking and why he seemed to be put in a position where he got shot so often.

When Nick embarked on this waltz through his own personal hell, he did not know that he was being watched and had been watched for a long, long time. Those who watched him knew everything about him; they even knew why he was doing this to himself now.

Nick Caldwell was a "just the facts" kind of guy. Every square peg had a square hole. He believed that logic, facts and evidence that could be codified and proven was all that mattered. He didn't believe in luck, chance, magic, a mystical world or coincidence. As for a spiritual world he didn't comment; his indoctrination as a kid prevented him from commenting on such things.

He did believe that spiritual things were fine for other people to believe in but not for him. He had no real problem with God, well accept maybe that he was still very angry that God allowed his family to be destroyed. He had no problem with God's kid either. He had a major problem with their communication apparatus...organized groups of so-called believers. Those believers who told him, "his children were in a better place," or that he needed to "move on," or those who said, "God has a plan" that we wouldn't be able to understand. He was adamant about his view of faith. One of Nick's major secrets was that he was a believer and that is why he was so hurt and felt so betrayed when he lost Mary and little Wil, his children, and when his wife Annie left him.

Those who had been watching him all this time usually didn't interfere, but they had concluded that subtlety would not work. There were three who lobbied the watchers and they fervently believed it was time for Nick Caldwell to get a "whack on the side of the head," and wake up and see the beauty in the world. Nick Caldwell didn't believe in beauty or the world. So, he decided the best way to deal with his feeling of hopelessness was not to disappear but to become invisible.

This is where the story begins, this was going to be Nick Caldwell's holiday hallucination.

Chapter 2

There were two terrible seasons for Nick, the holiday season starting with Halloween ending with New Years and the two months that included the dates of his children's deaths and their birthdays. Since their deaths he celebrated the holidays doing the things he did when his daughter was alive. He decorated, he was full of good cheer too, largely because he was usually full of good whiskey and sometimes the breakfast of champions, poached eggs, like his grandfather made, and potatoes, a staple in any Scot-Irish diet. Recently, however, he had traded hash browns for distilled potatoes with tomato juice, tabasco and just a little salt, a dash Toney's and a wee bit of lemon. After this breakfast he was ready for the new day of more self-indulgent self-pity and anger. He lived in an altered state of reality. He didn't mind this, in fact he barely noticed, he didn't believe that reality was all it was cracked up to be anyway.

He was a creature of habit and he did have a schedule:
Morning (starting at 10 am)
Get up
Feed Baron and Ruby and give them their dental stick
Let them out and bring them in
Have breakfast and his potato hangover health drink
Sit and sleep
Lunch (eat something around 2 pm))
Let Baron and Ruby out and bring them in
Sit and watch a movie with Baron and Ruby (Fridays they got to choose the movie)
Evening (starting around 5 pm)
Feed Baron and Ruby
Let Baron and Ruby out and bring them in
Dinner with his friends Mr. Jameson, Mr. Dewar and sometimes Mr. B. Trace. Eat something around 7 pm
Sit and watch a movie with Baron and Ruby or try to read if he could focus

Midnight, take Baron and Ruby for a clandestine walk with his friend, Mr. Glock. Get home, give Baron and Ruby a treat.

Pass out or fall asleep around 2:30 am.

Every other Friday he had his supplies delivered and Saturday was wash day. As far as personal hygiene, he made an effort to sit in his shower every day until his hot water ran out.

Such was the average day of Nick Caldwell, PI, crime fighter and budding alcoholic; after a while he didn't even have to take a drink to numb himself. The worst part of his days was remembering. He remembered almost everything in stark detail of his time with his daughter. He also remembered his dogs Duke and Tina. He remembered Starbuck, Bo, Samantha, Bella, Pixie all the way back to his first dogs, Inkie and Lucifer, his aunt's dog whom his family adopted when she was transferred. He always had a dog. He loved dogs because they were so much better than people, noble, honest and you always knew where you stood with them. He preferred their company far more than the company of people.

It was clear even to Nick that he was traveling a precarious road. It was clear that something needed to be done and it was clear whatever that was that needed to be done, Nick would probably not be the one to do it.

+

Nick had also meticulously planned several things to misdirect his friends and family so they would not bother him. He had led them to believe and that he and the pups had left Chicago and were somewhere in a cabin hide away in Michigan. He had rented a cabin in the Upper Peninsula but never left Chicago.

Nick Caldwell was a mess

.

Chapter 3

Bob was sitting outside hearing room 0791 with his witnesses. The sergeant at arms stood in front of the door.

"Do you know how long before we can go in?" Bob asked.

The sergeant replied sarcastically, "Could be in a few minutes, a few hours, a few days, a few months, a few years...or an eternity." This brought laughter from all the sergeants at arms standing in front of all the other hearing rooms.

"Wonderful, I have been assigned a hearing room with Don Rickles on watch," Bob said.

"Thank you, I like Don Rickles," the sergeant said.

"I only ask because I have an important case to discuss in there," Bob said.

"That's what they all say," the sergeant said.

"Would it make any difference if I told you that Pete put my request forward?" Bob asked.

The sergeant looked impressed, "Pete himself sent you here?"

"Yes," Bob said.

"Well, let me see." He looked at his list and smiled and looked up, and said, "Ah, I see." He laughed and said, "Nope makes no difference at all." Then he laughed again.

Bob sat down and huddled with his witnesses.

"I don't know how long this will take," Bob said.

A couple of his witnesses spoke up.

"We have an idea," Queenie said.

"We want to contact our friend to come over here and perhaps he can get a message into the hearing room," Duke said.

"Are you thinking of Sam?" Tina asked.

Her brother said, "Who else?" and smiled. "All of us were talking about this just the other day."

"All of you? Who?" Tina asked.

"Queenie said, "Don't know.""

Duke said, "You know."

Tina said, "I know?"

Duke said, "That's right."

Tina said, "That's right?"

Queenie said, "Absolutely correct."

"And of course, Sam was there too," Duke said.

"Do you really think Sam would help," Tina asked.

"Sure," Duke said. "All the three of us have to do is sit and think really hard about Sam and he will show."

Tina, Queenie and Duke began to think about Sam. In a matter of minutes, a man with white hair and large moustache wearing a white suit, smoking a pipe sauntered into the room. He waved at Duke and walked over. He politely bowed to Queenie and Tina.

He said, "Ladies, good afternoon. Duke, how are you today, old fella?"

"I'm good, Sam, thanks for asking," Duke said.

"How can I be of service?" Sam asked.

"We've been waiting a long while for our hearing and we would like to get in for our hearing," Tina said.

Sam looked perplexed, "What's stopping you?"

"See that man in front of the door?" Queenie said.

"Yes," Sam said.

"He is. He says it could be an eternity before we get in," Queenie said.

A small voice came from the bench Bob and two small children were sitting on.

"It's important, it's about our daddy," the little girl said.

"Well, let's see what we can do," Sam said.

Duke said, "I don't know, Sam, the sergeant at the door has been firm about not getting in until he decides that we get in."

"You know, Duke, the other night I was sitting with Morty..." Sam said.

"Morty?" Duke asked.

11

"You know Morty," Sam said. "Morty Friedman and I were discussing a situation just like this and he said that *'Hell hath no fury like a bureaucrat scorned,'* which is funny because we're here. Old Morty is right. Do you mind if I try something?" Sam asked.

"Not at all," Duke said.

Sam turned to Bob and said, "Excuse me, do you have a pen and some paper?"

"Yes, I do Mr. Clem…" Bob was interrupted.

"None of that Mr. stuff; just call me Sam, like everyone else here."

Sam sat on the bench and scribbled something on the paper, then showed it to Duke, Queenie and Tina.

"Good enough?" Sam asked.

"Perfect," Duke said.

Sam walked over to the sergeant at arms and said, "Hello, "I'm Sam…"

He was interrupted by the sergeant. "I know who you are, and I am pleased to meet you. You know we have a nickname for you."

Sam said, "I'm flattered, I would like to speak to you about…"

The sergeant interrupted again. "We call you Comet Man, get it?'

"I'm afraid I do," Sam said, "but I'd like to see if I could get my friends here into their hearing?"

"I'm sorry, Comet Man, but we have a procedure here," the sergeant said, "no exceptions."

"I understand, but remember the BOSS' kid said, *'Suffer little children to come unto me, and forbid them not: for of such is the kingdom of God."*

"Yes, I do," the sergeant said.

"Well, I think these may well be the little children he was speaking of and their friends," Sam said.

"That may be, sir, but we have rules and protocol," the sergeant said.

"Sergeant, how about this, could you take this note in and get it to Peter, so he can get it to the BOSS' kid?" Sam asked.

"It's a little unorthodox but maybe," the sergeant said, and then whispered, "if you could quote one of your favorite naughty things you wrote."

"I'd be happy to, let me see...how about this, *'Heaven for the climate, hell for the company.'*" The sergeant roared with laughter. Sam said, "or this one, *'I don't like to commit myself about **Heaven** and **Hell**; you see, I have friends in both places.'*"

The sergeant almost fell over laughing this time. "I would be honored to pass your note, Mr. Comet Man."

"Thank you kindly," Sam said.

Tina turned to Duke and asked, "What did he write on the note?"

Duke smiled and said, what else? *"Heaven goes by favor. If it went by merit, you would stay out and your dog would go in."*

Queenie and Tina smiled.

The sergeant entered hearing room 0791 and delivered the note. When he returned, he ushered Bob and his party into the room. As he shut the door, he waved to Sam who had started to head away from the hearing room. When Sam got outside, he noticed a very tall young man walking toward him. The young man was no stranger as they had talked several times about poetry.

They had an amiable discussion about a comment Sam had made about poetry. Sam called to the young man, "Neth, what are you doing around here?"

"Just taking a walk, how about you?" the Neth said.

"Oh, I was doing a favor for friends who were having trouble getting into their hearing room," Sam said.

"Don't tell me, hearing room 0791 with a rather officious sergeant at arms?" the Neth asked.

"You know him?" Sam asked.

13

The Neth answered, "Not really, but when I first got here, I attended a hearing and talked to the guy while I was waiting. Did he happen to tell you what he did for a living before he came here?"

"What was his profession?" Sam asked.

The Neth smiled. "He worked for the IRS."

Aghast, Sam said, "And he got in here? Shocking."

They both laughed.

"Neth, my boy, do you still want to discuss why I wrote, *'The poetry was all in the anticipation - there is none in the reality.'*"

"I do," the Neth said.

"May I suggest we go visit our friends from Bourbon country and discuss this thoroughly?"

"You may," the Neth said.

The two men walked off in conversation.

Chapter 4

Nick sat on the edge of his bed. He was awakened by a woodpecker from his afternoon nap and was working up the energy to go to the kitchen and feed Baron and Ruby and have the first cocktail of the evening not to be confused with his first cocktail of the afternoon, that he had a few hours ago.

He had been playing with the idea of writing his memoir; he thought it would be amusing, which it wouldn't be. He planned to call it, *I came, I failed, I got fucked up drunk*, by Nick Caldwell, Chicago's premier jerk off.

"Ahh," he said to himself, "there is nothing like Northern Michigan for solitude and quiet. It's a place to either pull yourself together or have a nervous breakdown...so what the hell, why not try both."

Ruby and Baron were not impressed with the cabin, except for the exceptionally large fireplace and a large bed. They constantly complained about everything else. Their idea of roughing it was a La Quinta or Quality Inn Suite, with TV, air conditioning, no bugs and restaurants that food could be brought back to the room. There were weird critters out here in the woods, and they had no desire to get to know any of them.

So, they spent their days watching his extensive collection of DVDs and listening to his extensive collection of Jazz CDs or as Baron put it "Jazz to pass out by."

Today, Baron thought he would open a conversation.

"How much longer are we going to have to do this Paul Bunyan thing?" he asked.

Ruby chimed in with, "Aren't we on Dante's fifth level of self-indulgent pity party?"

Nick, having just finished his second afternoon cocktail replied, "You do know I can hear you and I know that you are not really talking, it's all in my head."

"Usually, we would agree with you, but no, Nick, you are becoming so pathetic we decided we were actually going to have to speak up," Baron said. "We decided it was the only way to get your attention."

"You can't fool me, I know, I'm just making this up in my mind," Nick said.

"Wrong, gumshoe," Ruby said. "We are talking because we're the only ones up her to do an intervention."

"Funny," Nick said. "You can't fool me; I know you can't really talk. I'll show you I will make up what you will say next, okay, okay, you will say, 'do we have to watch the Thin Man movie again? I have all of Asta's line memorized.'"

"Wrong," Ruby said. "I was going to say that when we get back to Chicago, why don't you go pick out a nice refrigerator box and have it handy when you slip into homelessness or insanity, whichever comes first. I'm betting on insanity."

"Baroni, why is she talking down to me that way?" Nick said.

"Maybe because you are lying down on the floor," Baron said, "and no matter how much Mr. Carrandini would like to believe I am Italian, I am not, so until you start showering again and brushing your teeth…"

Ruby interrupted, "…and using deodorant and wearing clean clothes, we don't want to hear any endearing terms like Baroni or Rubaro."

"You guys are talking a lot. I must be Doctor Doolittle," Nick said, laughing, "I can talk to the animals."

"You are acting more like Doctor Dumbass or Do-nothing," Ruby said.

"I don't have to talk to you. There are literally hundreds, maybe thousands, of other animals around here I could talk to if I wanted to," Nick said, and pointed to the window, where a large grey squirrel was sitting looking in. "I'll talk to him." He turned to the window and said, "Hey Squirrel, old boy, keeping your nuts safe?" Nick rolled on the floor laughing, the squirrel shook his head. "Nick said, "What's the matter, possum got your nuts?"

In a deep baritone voice, the squirrel replied, "Hey, loser, why don't you get packed up and go back to Chicago and stop polluting our atmosphere up here?" Then the squirrel walked defiantly away from the window.

Nick laughed so hard, he passed out.

After he woke up and fed them and walked them and fell asleep on the couch for the night, Ruby went ad hopped on the bed and fell asleep.

Baron took his place at the other end of the couch from Nick. Before he drifted off to sleep, he prayed, "Duke, Queenie, Tina, Starbuck, Samantha, any of you up there that can hear me. I know that all dogs go to heaven, Nick has made us look at the movie enough times. I'm asking if you could talk to someone up where you are to see if there was a way to help Nick get back on track? We don't know what to do. Except for us, he thinks he is all alone. He's not; he has his family and his PI family. We're getting desperate. Ruby suggested that we call Maureen and ask her to talk some sense into him, and she said if Maureen couldn't, maybe she could shoot some sense in him. I thought that was a little extreme even for Ruby. Please help. Baron fell asleep and drifted to where all BearhounDs went when they slept, their cosmic plane where they figured things out. He became aware he was not alone; he raised his head and saw a tan dog with floppy ears that looked like the movie dog Benji on stilts and thirty pounds heavier.

"You know who I am?" the dog asked.

"I think so," Baron said. "You're Starbuck."

"Correct, kid," Starbuck said. "Your pop wanted to deliver this message, but tonight is Duke's mahjong night and he and Queenie, Tina and their friends Sam and Morty are going to listen to their friend the Neth, who is going to jam with Hendricks, Lennon, John not Karl...Karl didn't make it up here, George Harrison with Krupa on drums at 'The Saint's Came Marching Inn Club' tonight. There is even a rumor that King Cole, Aretha and Ella might drop in. Good deal, no cover tonight. So, he asked me to let you know they are on it and not to worry, okay? Well, gotta go, this is my softball night, and I'm playing second. You know who's on first?"

"Who?" Baron said.

"That's right, kid." Starbuck gave a big laugh. "Just kidding; we got Musial there tonight and get this, Clemente is in right and Campanella catching, cool huh?"

"Where do you play?" Baron asked.

"In heaven, kid. Where do you think we play, in Iowa or something?" Starbuck said with a little grin. "Get back to sleep, Baron, you're going to have some 'ruff' days ahead of you...see what I did there?"

"Yes, sir, funny, and thanks," Baron said. He yawned and fell back asleep.

Chapter 5

Bob presented the case to the tribunal.

The Chair of the Most High Tribunal stated, "Bob, it is our understanding that you are here to petition a divine intervention for one Nicholas Charles Caldwell, of the City of Chicago, State of Illinois, United States, located in the northern hemisphere of Earth, is that you correct?"

"It is," Bob said.

"Bob, you do understand that we get requests from this part of the Universe all the time and the success rate is very, very low. I remember that from that particular city and that particular state at least three or four of their elected, what they call governors, petitioned all the time and none of them learned their lesson very well."

"I am aware of that, Gabriel, but those were politicians," Bob said.

"Oh, that's right, what does Mr. Caldwell do?"

Duke spoke up. "He fights for truth, justice and the American way."

"Is Mr. Caldwell Superman, and who are you, may I ask?" Gabriel asked.

"Gabriel..." Duke was interrupted.

"I recognize you. You're Duke, that pup that jumped in front of your owner and sacrificed your own life to save him, correct?" Gabriel said.

"I am, Gabriel," Duke said.

"You know, Duke, that was an unselfish thing to do, particularly considering that you were close to the time of joining us. You didn't have to suffer that pain, you were already coming here, all of your kind come here....It is an honor to meet you , call me Gabe," he said.

"I did suffer but not as much as Nick has. He lost everything he loved and he still, although he was very angry with you, tried to right wrongs," Duke said.

"Who are those with you?" Gabe asked.

"This is my sister, Tina, Queenie who was a friend of Nick's, and Mary and William Caldwell," Duke said.

Gabe turned to Mary and William. "You are Mr. Caldwell's children that I read about in the file?"

Mary said, "We are, sir. We are here to ask you to help our daddy. After we, well you know, came here, my mom had trouble dealing with it and had to leave my dad. He has never really gotten over what happened, and it has hardened his heart, and we want him to move forward so someday he can come to be with William and me and all his other loved ones."

"I received letters from several pups, including one from Starbuck, Samantha and Bo, all former BearhounD Supreme Guides. I also received one from a new arrival from a man named Roy and another named Tim. In fact, every member of Tim's family that is here signed the letter. He also has support for this petition from someone called Uncle Joe and from a Kurt Murray and Tracy Donavon.

"We have also received a lot of prayers. Two of the clergy pray for Mr. Caldwell daily, an Episcopal priest," he looks at his notes," Lizzy and a Catholic priest, a Father Grey. My, there are a lot of people who seem to be concerned, a Katie, a Greg, Bart, Constance and a Felix, Nancy Drew?" Gabe turned to his clerk, "Is that right?"

"Yes, sir, she worked with Mr. Caldwell and he helped her get a position with the FBI and adopted her dog," the clerk replied.

"Here is a prayer from a Baron. He is the one that prayed for this hearing just last night. He is mentioned in Starbuck's letter, a fine pup and a good Mahjong player," Gabe said. "His family all pray for him; he's a lucky man. Bob, can you explain why some of these people are so dedicated to Mr. Caldwell?"

"I can," Bob said. "Roy was his former partner that inadvertently was partially responsible for him losing his family. Tim is someone wrongly accused of a crime and died for it and Nick cleared his name. Mr. Murray and Ms. Donavon

20

were murdered, and Nick found those responsible after forty years. Uncle Joe is the Uncle of Mr. Joey Carrandini..."

"The Bat?" Gabe asked.

"The same," Bob said.

"That's one who has a lot of work to do, including trying to get that brother of his on the straight and narrow," Gabe said. "How did Mr. Caldwell help him?"

"Found Uncle Joe's murderer," Bob said.

"I see," Gabe said. "There are some parts of his record we will discuss in private that pertain to his work." M.D. turned to the other two members of the Tribunal, Peter, Michael?"

"I have seen nothing in his professional record that is troubling, his motives are usually very righteous. The only thing that troubles me is that he gets into positions where it is almost like he wants to get hurt or shot," Michael said, "but all in all, if I were going into battle I would want someone like him on our side."

"Pete?" Gabe asked.

"He's a good man in a lot of pain and like most men, he is flawed. He has a hard exterior, but beneath that he is a good man. He is unafraid," Peter said.

"Is there anything else, Bob?" Gabe asked.

"Yes, there is another witness that would like to be heard. You have that request, Gabriel," Bob said.

"I do?" Gabe asked. The clerk handed him the witness form; Gabe gave a little smile. "Since you are aware of this request, you must know that this witness would like to be heard in private."

"I am aware, and we have no objection," Bob said.

Duke gave a little low grumble.

"Duke, are you okay with this?

"Gabriel, may I have a moment to confer with Duke?" Bob asked.

"You may, he has earned the Tribunal's consideration," Gabe said.

Bob leaned over to Duke and whispered into his ear.

Duke wagged his tale and said, "I'm good."

Gabe smiled and said, "Yes you are, you always have been, and you have always been just a little cranky. I've always liked that. The Tribunal is adjourned while we deliberate." Gabriel, Michael and Peter retired to the deliberation chamber.

Chapter 6

The deliberation chamber was much smaller that the hearing room. It had a small conference table and four chairs. Gabriel took the spot at the head of the table, Peter at the end of the table and Michael sat at Gabriel's left, at his right sat the witness.

"Hello J. It is my understanding that you have something to add?" Gabriel said.

J. smiled, "How about that Duke, huh, and those kids were adorable."

"Yes, they were," Gabriel said. "What do you have to add?"

"First, I want to talk about Nick's great family. I was sitting in the back with his mom, cool lady. She told me of all her children Nick was the most introspective and very hard on himself. His younger brothers and sisters adore him, his older brother loves him more than Nick would ever guess. He has a lot of people who love him here and there," J said.

"His father is a perfectionist and was hard on Nick and still is, but he does it out of love. Billy, his dad, was a cop and a good one, but he held both his older brother and Nick to a very strict standard. Gave him a sense of honor and duty, pressed Nick to overcome his fear and be courageous, things that were scary, dangerous and painful." J. turned to Gabriel and said, "You get that, don't you?"

Gabriel said, "Are you going to ever let that go?"

"Hey, I'm not complaining, and there is no reproach in the statement, I'm just saying," J. said. "I can relate. That is why I'm urging you guys to grant the divine intervention."

"Do you have any evidence to support this request? Gabriel. said.

"I do," J. said, "and I have a plan. I know how you are all about this free will thing and I agree, but sometimes you need to give people a little nudge."

"Let's hear what he has to say," Michael said.

23

"I'm interested in his plan," Peter said.

"What have you got, Son?" Gabriel said.

"Cool," J. said. "After he lost his family, he didn't lose his faith even though he renounced it. Every night I listened to him tell me how ticked off he was and how he would never believe again, he would never pray again, he would never trust again. Wow, some of the things he called us, well I don't want to repeat."

"We've heard it all before, not a big deal. An emotional reaction to a tragic situation, we understand that," Gabriel said.

"But he really believed he meant it, but he kept on trying to do good," J. said. "He never wavered. He wasn't happy, his heart wasn't filled with forgiveness, even though I would whisper to him that he might not believe in us, but we still believed in him. I stopped doing that because he would wake up in the morning and be even more angry."

"Why do you do things like that?" Gabriel asked.

"Cause," J. said.

"Cause?" Gabriel repeated. "How about cause, why?"

J. smiled, "Because I like him. He fights for the little guys, for justice, for those who have lost hope, for those who are forgotten and not because he has been taught to do that but because it is who he is, and it is how he is made. He doesn't get this, but he is wired to do what's right. He doesn't care who someone is, if you need his help, he is there. He has provided a life for two kids, Katie and Greg. He came along at a time when this old cantankerous detective was considering eating his gun. Nick didn't know that, but he was there at the right time. He's partly responsible why 'Joey the Bat' has stayed on the straight and narrow. Joey doesn't want to disappoint Nick and now Joey is also trying to do good. Antonio, different story, but at least when he does bad, he thinks he is doing it for good reasons."

"Would you like to clarify that last part about Antonio?" Gabriel asked.

J. smiled, "No, Antonio is a work in progress, but if we don't help Nick, Antonio is a lost cause."

"Anything else?" Michael asked.

"Yes, when Nick captured the Charlotte who was responsible for Tim MacCarty's execution, to defend that Episcopal priest, Lizzy and himself, her sister, who was headed down a bad path, vowed to kill Nick."

Peter said, "So?"

"After a few years dealing with Nick, she cleaned up her act. She doesn't want to kill the guy who had to shoot her sister, but she's in love with Nick and she, get this, it's really cool, prays for him every night. I think she wants to care and protect him," J. said.

"I have a question," Michael said. "Doesn't Nick think he's Sam Spade?"

"No," J. said. "He thinks sometimes that he is Nick Charles from the *Thin Man*, but how many people that have made it here thought they were Napoleon or Joan of Arc?"

Gabriel said, "Don't let Dashiell Hammett know or he'll try to sue him. Okay, what's the plan?"

"Nick loves Christmas; he just likes the feeling. When he was kid, he would write a letter to Santa and try to send a birthday card here," J. said. "Here's the plan and I have spent a lot of time working on it. Here is what we do. We send Bob to work on Nick, but we also send a Christmas Angel who is supposed be a department store Santa, but he is really bad at it."

"And," Gabriel says.

"We have Bob doing his guardian angel thing and Nick trying to reform bad Santa, you know, like in that Capra movie when Clarence went to Bedford Falls," J. said.

"That was a movie," Peter said.

"You are not seeing the big picture, Pete. We send our bad Santa and Nick straightens him out, and Bob straightens Nick out. It will be great. Trust me, by Christmas Nick will be full of the spirit of Christmas," J. said.

25

"Who do you have in mind for your bad Santa?" Gabriel asked. "Did you contact the Christmas Angels and ask for candidates?"

"I did and there lies the rub," J. said. "I mentioned they would have to go to Chicago in December and work with a private detective who is featured in a series of detective novels. Some of them had read the books and word spread fast," J. said.

"And...?" Gabriel asked.

"There were many who declined," J. said.

"How many?" Michael asked.

"All but one," J. said

"What?" Gabriel asked.

"We should work on this. Some have real prejudices against private eyes. Some just hated the books; they said dogs talked in the books," J. said. "Some didn't like the weather, none of them like the traffic."

"Did you remind them that dogs talk here?" Gabriel asked.

"I did, but no go," J. said.

"Who was the one who said he would go?" Peter said.

"I think you all know him," J. said

"Stop stalling, who is it?" Gabriel said.

"Cuthbert, although he was quite on top of his game," J. said.

"CUTHBERT!!" all three yelled.

"He was a drunk, smoked cigars and cursed his entire life. He is and was delusional and not very nice and you're going to send him?" Gabriel demanded. "We only made him a Christmas angel because there was nowhere to put him."

"But, he has deep down a very, very good heart," J. said.

Gabriel smiled. "He does, before he came here, he would rescue animals and he would use his food money to feed them. He would panhandle to get money to take them to the vet. He had dogs and cats, a few mice, birds. The man loves

26

animals. We never figured out how he was able to care for all of them and still have enough money for whisky."

Michael said, "He also did not like people at all, unless you were a bartender."

"That is why he is perfect, he and Nick have a lot in common," J. said.

"Have you discussed this plan with Bob?" Peter asked.

J. smiled, "I did, and he is all for it."

"Did you tell him that Cuthbert was going with him?" Peter asked.

"I thought it would be better to wait until the plan was approved," J. said.

Gabriel sighed, "Okay, let's vote, I have to get over to the Saints Go Marching Inn tonight. Krupa asked me to come over and jam tonight and I have to go and get my horn."

+

J. walked out of the deliberation chamber and Bob was waiting.

"What's the verdict?" Bob asked.

J. gave him a big smile. "It's a go!"

They gave each other a high five.

"Who's the Christmas angel?

J. said, "Hey, let's talk about it over supper. I have a great idea, let's go to supper and go over to the Calvin Center. They have Movie Monster COM over there tonight, and I'm going to meet my buddy Drew. I'm telling you, nobody, and I mean nobody, knows more about monster movies than he does. I heard that Boris Karloff, Bella Lugosi and Vincent Price are going to be in the autograph booth tonight, how about it."

"Sure, sounds like fun," Bob said.

Later that evening, Bob, Drew and J were watching a screening of *Halloween*, and the audience was really into it. Halfway through, the audience gave out a terrifying scream and no one screamed louder than Bob. J. had just told him that Cuthbert would be going to Chicago with him for Christmas.

27

Chapter 7

After the movie Bob left Movie Monster COM and sat alone in a back booth at the Heavenly Hashtag Java Hut. He ordered a cup of St. Joe with sugar and a long St. John pastry. He was trying to figure out how he was going to help Nick with a "side kick" like Cuthbert, the Cranky Christmas Angel, for that matter the crankiest angel in the entire Host of Angels.

Cuthbert was universally recognized as a humbug, cantankerous, most difficult angel around. Everyone wondered how he got past the gate. The only beings that greeted him when he arrived were scores of dogs, cats, hamsters, rodents, squirrels and every other kind of animals that roamed the planet. He was beloved by them. When he resided on earth he wore a t-shirt that read *"Dogs Because People Suck."* He also had a sign in the hovel he lived in that proclaimed, *"Dogs, Cats and other Animals Welcome, Humans Tolerated but not often or for long."* It was homemade. He smoked a pipe but preferred cigars because they were more offensive. He had a mat in front of his front and back door that read, *"GO AWAY."* To say he was unpleasant would be a compliment.

There were stories that he hadn't always been that disagreeable, but no one believed them. He drank, smoked, cussed and sometimes demonstrated behavior that shocked his next-door neighbors. One time a neighbor hurt one of his dogs and he stood in his backyard and screamed for the neighbor to come out so that he could do to him what the neighbor had done to his dog. He yelled *"Get your cowardly ass out here so I can kick it!"* It was generally believed that he was crazy. He fostered that belief so no one would bother him.

This is the Christmas angel that Bob was going to have to work with to try to restore the Spirit of Christmas and rekindle the faith of Nick Caldwell.

He believed working with Cuthbert would be like swimming the Atlantic Ocean pulling Noah's Ark loaded with animals.

As he read the plan that was developed, he had no idea how he could implement it. He knew, being Nick's Guardian Angel, what he was supposed to do. The plan called for Cuthbert to get a job as a mall Santa and somehow make Nick's acquaintance and bring forth the holiday cheer.

He read the information on Nick. It gave a complete picture of Nick's entire life. Bob knew all this because he had been with Nick from the beginning. Nick wasn't the same person that he protected in the early years. Nick hardened, he was cynical, he was separated from his family and didn't spend much time with his friends, all of whom were connected to his work. He also had become a recluse to some extent with the exception of his two dogs. It wasn't that he didn't care about his family and friends; he did but he just didn't want to be around anyone.

Bob was going to have to come up with a way to connect Nick with Cuthbert, but how. He doubted Nick would be going to the mall to see Santa.

Bob was tired and decided to go rest before he had to go to the Christmas Village to see Cuthbert. The cranky angel was the only one in that community that didn't decorate.

As Bob walked home, he was trying to figure out how he was going to pull this off. Then it came to him, Nick liked movies; he particularly liked detective mysteries and Christmas movies. He even watched Hallmark and Lifetime Christmas movies. Bob had what probably was a divine inspiration; he would design this intervention borrowing things from Christmas movies and stories.

When he arrived home, he opened the door and there was an envelope that someone had slid under his door. He opened it and read it; his heart sank.

Dear Bob,

I can't tell you how much it is appreciated that you are going to take on this task. We all want you to know that we will support and help in any way we can. Just reach out if you need to, whenever you need to.

Peace be with you, dude.

Your Pal,

J.

P. S. Nick needs to make a change of his own free will, so you and Cuthbert have to reveal who you are and what you are doing there to him. Hey, he talks to his dogs and they talk back, how hard will it be to convince him you guys are angels.

Bob read the note again and said to himself out loud, "It's a Wonderful Life."

Chapter 8

Bob arranged to meet Cuthbert at the Mother Teresa Café. He sat outside and waited for Cuthbert. About a half hour after the time the meeting was set, he sauntered up to the table accompanied by seven dogs he had met on the way: Junior and Fred, Golden Retrievers ; Inky, a Cocker; Bella, a Yorkie; Susie, a Scottie: and Inkie, a mop.

"You Bob?" Cuthbert said.

"Looks like a Bob to me," Junior said.

"What kind of angel are you?" Susie asked.

Bob looking tired already said, "I'm a Guardian Angel."

"You like the work?" Raphael asked.

"Of course he likes the work," Inky and Inkie said in unison. "Why would he do it, if he didn't like it?"

"Who do you guard?" Bella asked.

"That's not important," Bob said, clutching prayer beads.

"If it doesn't matter, then why in the name of the other place am I wasting my time this morning. I have things to do," Cuthbert said. "I have a lunch date with Frank to feed some birds."

"I didn't mean it like that, for His sake. I meant we have a job to do and we need to talk about that privately," Bob said, with slight irritation.

"We going to get breakfast or what?" Junior asked.

"Yea, we are. Why don't you all get one of those short tables over there and order, tell the server that it's on him," Cuthbert said, pointing at Bob.

"Cool," Raphael said. "They have eggs St. Benedict here right?

"I think so," Fred said.

"Cool, do you think they have Scotch Eggs?" Susie asked.

"I want a waffle," Bella said.

As Cuthbert's friends ordered, Cuthbert sat down with Bob.

"So, what do you want?" Cuthbert asked.

"You have been assigned to help me on a project," Bob said.

"Why?" Cuthbert asked.

"Because we need your particular talent," Bob said.

"What talent is that, being the only pissed off being up here?" Cuthbert said.

"What do you have to be all pissed off about?" Bob said.

"I'm here sitting across from you and I have to work on a dumb ass project with you; that's enough to piss off a saint," Cuthbert answered.

"What better things do you have to do?" Bob asked.

"I could be spending more time with them," Cuthbert pointed to the table of pups, "but I'm going to have to spend some time with a goody two-wings dumb ass like yourself."

"Who say's I'm dumb ass?" Bob said with an air of indignance.

Cuthbert looked down and said to the table of dogs. "If there is a dumb ass near here, point at them."

All the dogs pointed at Bob and then broke into laughter.

"You thought that was funny," Bob said.

"No, they thought it was funny," Cuthbert said.

"If you don't want to do this, then you're the one that can go tell Michael and Gabriel," Bob said.

"Why would I want to tell them," Cuthbert said.

"Because they are the ones, along with Peter, that chose you for this job," Bob said.

"Is the Michael we're talking about, is he the big guy with the sword that kicked all those other angels out a while back?" Cuthbert said. "A long while ago, he was like the Big Guy's hitman."

"The Big Guy doesn't have hitmen. Michael is an Archangel, not a hitman," Bob said. "Why would you say that?"

I don't know, you hear stuff," Cuthbert said. "Hey, what do you want from me. I'm from Chicago."

Bob said, "What did you say?"

Cuthbert repeated, "You hear things...."

"Not that," Bob said, "the other thing."

"Oh, what do you want, I'm from Chicago," he said.

Bob asked, "You're from Chicago?"

"Yep, what a great city. I wonder if the 'Monsters of the Midway' are still playing? Boy, that Halas is a great coach," Cuthbert said.

The table of dogs yelled out, "Da Bears."

"No, he isn't," Bob said.

"How do you know?" Cuthbert asked.

"Well, if you ever got out from under wherever you live, you would know that Coach Halas is up here," Bob said.

"You know, after I got here, I would check in on the Bears, the Cubs, even the Sox, but it made me home sick," Cuthbert said.

"Well, congratulations you just won a round trip to Chicago, in the winter." Bob smiled.

Cuthbert's eyes lit up for a moment, then he looked sad. "I guess I wouldn't know anyone there now."

"Probably not, did you have any family there?" Bob asked.

"No one that would be there now, I guess," Cuthbert said. "What's the job?"

"I am the Guardian Angel of a man who is in trouble, and needs help," Bob said.

"Why am I not surprised at that," Cuthbert replied.

"That's not funny," Bob said.

"It's a little funny," he said.

"May I continue?" Bob replied. "He is a good man who has lost his way...."

Cuthbert sang, "Bah, Bah, Bah…, you have to admit that was funny."

If an angel could glare, Bob did.

"What's this guy's name?" Cuthbert asked.

"Nick Caldwell, he's a private detective, lost his family, never adjusted, almost a hermit. He has lost his spirit for life and Christmas and we are going to help him get it back," Bob said, proudly.

"What do mean, lost his family?" he asked.

Bob answered, "They were murdered when he was a cop and his wife left not long after."

"And we're going to make it all better?" he said.

"That's the job," Bob said.

"Are you freakin' crazy? How are we going to turn him into Mr. Holiday Jolly? We can't fix something like that, I'm not sure it's possible," he said.

Bob was quiet. "I know but we have to try; that's all we can do. It is the wish of his daughter and son. They asked me to ask the Tribunal to try. Even his dog prayed for it."

"His dog? He has a dog?" Cuthbert asked.

"He has two, both rescues," Bob said.

"What was his name again?"

"Nick Caldwell," Bob said.

"Is he from the northside?" Cuthbert asked.

Bob looked at the file, "Yes."

"What were the names of his great Grandfather?" Cuthbert asked.

Bob shuffled some papers, "Andrew Robert Caldwell; hey, he was a cop too."

"I knew him, he wasn't one of those jerk cops, after my, well after I had troubles and started well… misbehaving, he would let me sleep it off in the back of one of the stores on his beat. He brought me food and let my dogs stay with me. He treated me like a person not some bum. He even tried to get me a job, but it didn't take. He tried, he really tried. I asked him how I could repay him, he just smiled and said with that thick Scottish accent, "I'm fine but maybe one day, lad."

Both angels were silent.

"Well," Bob said, "you better get going and get ready, we're leaving tonight. You have to be there tomorrow morning you have an interview."

"Interview," Cuthbert said.

"Yeah, you're going to be hired as a Santa at the mall," Bob said, with a very big smile.

"A what?" he asked. "No fu…"

"Cuthbert! Watch the adjectives," Bob said.

"No way, I can't play Santa. The real Santa doesn't even like me," Cuthbert said.

"You'll be fine," Bob said.

Bob was getting ready to leave when Junior walked up with a piece of paper in his mouth that he put in Bob's hand. "Thanks for breakfast, they take Arc Cards or Halleluiah Express."

Bob looked at Junior and smiled. "You're welcome."

Junior said, "And sorry about that dumb ass stuff."

"No problem," Bob said, as he watched Cuthbert walk away with his glorious posse of pups.

Chapter 9

Bright and early Bob had Cuthbert at one of the largest malls in Chicagoland. He was dressed in a red sport jacket and matching vest; grey trousers and he wore a green tie. He had a camel overcoat with a red, green and white striped scarf. He already had a long white beard and a head full of white hair. To set the ensemble off he wore oval wire rim glasses. Cuthbert was absolutely mortified.

He sat in the reception room with Bob, waiting for his interview.

"Now remember," Bob said, "first impressions are important, so try to hold it together, okay?"

"I feel like Christmas threw up all over me," he said.

"You look great. If you can just be polite for twenty minutes, you'll get the job, trust me," Bob said. "Answer the questions and try to look at the very least pleasant."

A tall man with a dark suit and a pleasant smile walked out and asked, "Mr. Quigle?"

Bob nudged Cuthbert. "That's me."

"I'm John Wiley, please come in and let's chat."

Cuthbert rose and looked like he was walking to the gallows.

"Have seat," said Wiley.

Cuthbert said, "Are you?"

"Am I what, Mr. Quigle?"

"Wiley," Cuthbert said.

For a moment, Wiley looked confused, then got a big smile on his face. "A sense of humor, that's wonderful. Santa has to have a sense of humor to get through the season."

Now Cuthbert looked confused and wondered is this guy an idiot?

"So, Mr. Quigle, what kind of Santa experience do you have?" Wiley asked.

"Well, I have seen *Miracle on 34th Street* and *The Santa Claus* several times," Cuthbert said.

Wiley almost fell out of his chair laughing.

Cuthbert was now convinced this guy is an idiot.

"You are a very funny man, Mr. Quigle, I like you," Wiley said. "What other experience do you have?"

"I know Santa," Cuthbert said.

Laughing, Wiley said, "Really?"

"Yeah, he doesn't like me," Cuthbert replied.

Wiley couldn't stop laughing... "doesn't like you, that's great."

"Mr. Quigle, you are amazing," Wiley said.

"One last question, do you like children?" Wiley asked.

"I don't understand the question," Cuthbert said.

"Well, you will be working around children in this position," Wiley asked.

"Right, so are you asking whether I like children as individuals or as a group?"

"Wiley seemed delighted and started laughing again. "That's good."

"Actually, I like dogs better," Cuthbert said.

Wiley burst out laughing again. "Me too, I like my dog better than my own kids," Wiley said, roaring. "Mr. Quigle, you're hired and welcome to the mall. You start work the Monday before Thanksgiving. That will give you a chance to meet the photographer and the elves unless you are bringing your own elves?"

"Was I supposed to?" Cuthbert said.

"You're great," Wiley said. "I am looking forward to this Christmas season working with you. Before you go, go down to Human Resources to get payroll set up and your employee Identification card. It was great to meet you, Mr. Quigle. When you come in on Monday, come by and say hello. Glad you're on board. See you then."

Cuthbert walked out of Wiley's office looking dazed.

"What happened?" Bob asked.

"I'm not sure," Cuthbert said.

Bob asked, "Did you get the job?"

"Yeah, I start on the Monday before Thanksgiving," Cuthbert said.

"That's great," Bob said.

Cuthbert still looked a little dazed.

"What's wrong?" Bob asked.

"I'm not sure," Cuthbert said, "but whatever meds that guy Wiley is on, I want some. You wouldn't know how far we are from Blackies, do you?"

"Cuthbert, I got some bad news," Bob said.

"What?" He asked.

"Blackies closed a few years ago," Bob said.

"Last night I was in heaven, and now I feel I have been condemned to everlasting suffering in hell."

Chapter 10

Bob sat on the couch, reading the paper, when Cuthbert stumbled downstairs. "You know when you start your job you won't be able to stay up all night watching old movies."

"Don't you think it's a little creepy for us to be staying in Caldwell's house while he is up in the north boonies?" Cuthbert said.

"No, this gives you the opportunity to get to know the man," Bob said.

"I think I have a good take on him," Cuthbert said.

"Oh really, you've been here twenty-four hours and you have a good take on him," Bob said, with more than a hint of disbelief.

"Yep," Cuthbert said. "You know, Bobby boy, I was a bum, and I was poor because I was a drunk and I messed up every decent thing I had when I was here, but I wasn't stupid, just angry."

Bob said, "I'm sorry Cuthbert, I didn't mean to hurt your feelings..."

"You didn't, Bobby boy. You never lived here, you've always been an angel, you've never been cold or hungry, you never had a bet. Your whole existence has been up there, and I bet when you came here to be Nick's guardian angel, you looked down just a tiny bit on him and everyone here. You have never been human; if you're interested in knowing, it is difficult and borders on sucking big time," Cuthbert said.

"I know it is difficult for them, that's why I...that's why we try to help and protect," Bob said, "and don't call me 'Bobby boy,' I really don't like it."

"I know, Bobby boy," Cuthbert said, with a big smile.

"That's it," Bob exclaimed.

"What?" Cuthbert said.

"You smiled and you have a great smile. You have to do that when you play Santa," Bob said.

39

"Bobby boy, shove it," he replied, with an even bigger smile.

"Fine, let's hear your assessment of Nick," Bob said, certainly in a challenging way, particularly for an angel.

Cuthbert smiled and said, "Okay, Bobby boy." Bob winced, and Cuthbert continued, "Nick grew up like a typical Scot-Irish kid or any of the Catholic kids who grew up on the north or southside whose parents were working stiffs. His old man was a cop, just like the rest of his family, or on his mother's side of the family there are cops and some that are even lawyers. I guess when Nick's time comes, he won't be running into those relatives up there.

"He went to Catholic schools through high school. His parents sacrificed to send all of his siblings to Catholic school, not realizing that sending a kid to Catholic school almost ensures they will eventually become a fallen away Catholic."

"Don't you think that is a bit of an overstatement?" Bob asked.

"Do you?" Cuthbert countered.

"Go on," Bob said.

Cuthbert continued, "He fell in love with his high school sweetheart; he chose to postpone college to Join the Chicago Police Department...just like Daddy. The problem was his big brother was already a cop and in his daddy's eyes no one could compare with the first-born son. He was from a Celtic family, his father was one generation from the old country, and they still thought like immigrants. That's not bad, not bad at all, but there is a plan for Celtic families and Nick screwed up and didn't follow it."

"How so?" Bob asked.

"There were five kids," Cuthbert said.

"Wrong," Bob said, with satisfaction.

"Nope, I'm right," Cuthbert said.

"No, you're wrong. There is Wil, three years later Nick arrived, then four years later Phil and two years later there was Laura. No, you're wrong," Bob insisted.

"Nope. you forgot one," Cuthbert said.

"Who did I forget?" Bob asked.

"You're a guardian angel, aren't you supposed to know this stuff?" Cuthbert said.

"I do know this stuff, but he is a person that has had more than one guardian angel. I got Nick when he was five; Malik had Nick for the first four years," Bob said.

"Malik, is he the guy who is in charge of the Trinity Raceway?" Cuthbert asked.

"Yeah, so what?" Bob said.

"I only been there once, I went to see Earnhardt race when Dave Pearson first arrived," Cuthbert said.

"I don't know who they are," Bob said.

"Of course, you don't," Cuthbert said. "Anyway, you missed one Caldwell kid."

"Okay, I'll bite, who?" Bob asked.

"You missed the first child, born ten years before Wil and thirteen years before Nick," Cuthbert said.

"You are crazy," Bob said.

"Nope, I'm informed," Cuthbert said.

"Okay, what's the child's name?" Bob said.

"Mary," Cuthbert said.

"That's Nick's daughter," Bob said, showing his irritation.

"It's his sister too," Cuthbert said.

"How do you know this?" Bob asked.

"When I heard that Andrew, Nick's grandfather, was joining us, I looked him up to thank him for his kindness. He was worried and concerned about his son Billy, who just shortly before Andrew passed on had thrown his daughter out because she was, shall we say, a 'wild child.' She left when she was eighteen, and they never heard from her again. She was thirteen when Nick was born, and she looked after him until Billy and she got into it and she left," Cuthbert said.

"Where is she now," Bob asked.

"No one knows...except the Big Guy and J., but you know that free will thing gets in the way. Why do you think he named his daughter Mary and his son, William?" Cuthbert said. "Now you know the Caldwells' most painful secret. Billy was not an easy guy to deal with sometimes. Remember, Phil and Laura moved away too."

"Do Phil and Laura know they have an older sister?" Bob asked.

"Nope, that secret was kept by Nick's mom, Billy, Wil and Nick. I'm pretty sure like most family secrets it was made clear that some things you never share with outsiders," Cuthbert said.

"What about uncles and aunts, cousins, friends?" Bob asked.

"You don't get it. Family secrets are sacred. You don't talk about them and if you do, only with some family members, not all," Cuthbert said.

"Do you think, Nick, being a detective has looked for her?" Bob asked.

"I do," Cuthbert said.

"Why do you think that?" Bob asked.

"Because, since Nick was in high school, he's kept a diary. They are all in his office; I read them last night." Cuthbert smiled.

"That's terrible," Bob said.

"Hey, Bobby boy, I was the one that pointed out staying here without Nick's permission was creepy, if you remember," Cuthbert said.

"You invaded his privacy," Bob almost bellowed.

"You've invaded his life for close to forty years," Cuthbert said."

"My job was to look after him," Bob said.

"And you have done a crackerjack job. He lost his children and his wife, he has been shot several times, he has become embittered and you let his only real friend, Duke, get shot and then he runs into the woman who's sister he killed,

42

and they are attracted to each other, and you probably whisper in his ear telling him she's a bad person, nothing could work with her..." Cuthbert said.

Bob shouted, "We don't interfere...Free Will...Get IT?

"Well, maybe you should, maybe you shouldn't be so fuckin' pious and help sometimes?" Cuthbert shouted back. "I wish my guardian angel helped me a little, maybe I might have straightened up and known my daughter and maybe I have grandkids."

Bob was shocked. "Angels don't use that kind of language. Cuthbert, you have...."

"Bobby boy, stuff it," Cuthbert said.

The phone rang. Bob and Cuthbert looked at each.

"Should we answer it?" Bob asked.

"You're asking me?" Cuthbert said. "The caller name is blocked, go ahead."

Bob gently picked up the phone, put it on speaker and said, "Hello?"

"Hey, Dudes, you need to play nice and lighten up...don't make me come down there...kidding. This morning has been interesting, but you have a job to do, so get going. Gotta go."

Chapter 11

Very little was said on the way to upper Michigan and the cabin where Nick had disappeared to, why no one really knew, probably including Nick.

For years all he had done was focus on his daughter and his soon-to-be son's murder. The people responsible were on their way to prison or on their way to hell. He loved his family and his extended family. He liked being a detective, he loved Chicago even with all its flaws, but he didn't want to be there, and he didn't want to be around anyone with the exception of Baron and Ruby, even though Ruby was getting sassier every day.

Nick knew that one day there would be a knock on the door. After all, most of the people he knew were detectives or were people who knew how to find other people for less than noble reasons. He looked at the calendar every morning and he wanted to go home to see the family for the Big Four holidays--Halloween, Thanksgiving, Christmas and New Year's. This was the only time of year everybody seemed to be around, even Sinclair Stewart, the detective from New Orleans came up to visit, whether there was a case or not. His sister Laura and her husband Bob Wilson and their twins and even some of the St. Louis staff would come up.

Nick figured one crisp morning there would be pounding on the door and it would be Sinclair or Bart or Phil or Katie and Greg, telling him to get his ass back to Chicago. So far though they had given him space and he was grateful to have the time.

He was not really pondering large life decisions, he was zoning out, spending time with the pups, watching movies, reading, and sleeping. He wasn't watching any news or listening to anything but music and selected podcasts.

Somedays he would go for long walks and think. Nick was trying to figure out where to go from here. He knew he didn't want to do corporate detective work unless there was an art heist. He always liked Steve McQueen in *The Thomas Crown Affair*. He wanted to be a gumshoe and he wanted to do cases that no one else would touch. Nick never had a lot of money but thanks to his business partner and best friend Bart Cheswick, he was comfortable enough to do those kinds of cases. Bart, the psychologist who spoke to the dead, turned security and investigative business mogul, kept the corporate side humming and Bart's husband was a big wheel now with 'Da Bears,' so he always had good seats at Soldier's Field.

As he examined his life, he really didn't know why he was so down or what he felt was missing. He wondered how could he feel serene and anxious at the same time? How could he feel good and have a feeling of dread at the same time? But he did.

He thought that maybe when he headed back to Chicago, he'd make an out-of-the-way stop in Ann Arbor, as he always liked going there. Maybe he would get Ronnie Silk and Mo Jones to meet him for dinner, since he had ducked out of going to Detroit to talk about a potential case.

It was late afternoon and he had finished feeding Baron and Ruby and letting them in and out. They were sitting on the couch watching a movie, *The Dark Knight,* with the real Batman, Christian Bale, when there was a knock on the door.

Baron and Ruby were on alert and Nick took his friend Mr. Glock out from under the cushion of the couch. He looked out the door and saw two of the weirdest looking people he had ever seen, one looked like an accountant, the other like Santa Claus.

He opened the door and gave the classic Nick Caldwell greeting, "Who the fuck are you and what do you want?" He gave this salutation holding his gun where they couldn't help but notice it was pointed at them.

Bob responded first, "You are Nick Caldwell."

"And you must be the guy who is going to get shot by Nick Caldwell," Nick said.

"Nick, we're here to just talk," Bob said.

"Who the hell are you?" Nick said.

Cuthbert responded, "You don't know me? I'm the fucking Fuller Brush man."

Nick almost smiled. "Why do you look like Santa?"

"Why do you look like an asshole whose been on a week-long bender?" Cuthbert asked.

"Funny," Nick said.

"Hey, listen butt head, I had to ride eight hours in a car with this asshole to find you. It's cold, are you going to invite us in or am I going to have to get Rudolph to kick your ass?" Cuthbert said. "Besides, I have to pee."

Nick opened the door and motioned them in, pointing with his gun.

"You know," Cuthbert said, "only a real fuck head would hold Santa at gun point. Where's your john?"

Nick pointed to the bathroom and watched Santa disappear.

All this time Ruby and Baron were wagging their tails and wiggling their butts. Nick looked at them and said, "Some watch dogs."

Cuthbert walked out of the bathroom. "What kind of degenerate are you? You keep hooch in the bathroom? Does Santa need to bring you a list of meetings of Bill W's Friends for Christmas? Mind if I smoke? Good." He pulled out a very large cigar and lit it.

Nick watched, a little dismayed.

Bob broke the silence. "Nick, we're here to help you. It's a little hard to explain, but many people who love you have prayed that you..."

Cuthbert interrupted, "For God's sake, literally." He laughed a little. "We're here to straighten your sorry ass out. People are worried about you. I can see that you are a no bullshit kind of guy, which is funny because you are absolutely so full of crap I'm surprised you can see."

"Is this supposed to be cheering me up, because if you are, you suck at this.?" Nick said.

"What Cuthbert is trying to say..." Bob said.

"Bob, shut the hell up, I got this. The sooner he gets this, the sooner we go home."

"What looney bin are you guys from?" Nick asked.

"I'll get to that," Cuthbert said. "Now, shut up and listen, I am going to give it to you straight. Now you won't believe it, but it's true. So, don't interrupt and I should tell you that that gun will do you no good. Are you ready? Or are you going to be an asshole about this?"

"I'm curious, go on. I can always shoot you later," Nick said.

"When I finish, I expect you will need a drink and I know I will," Cuthbert said.

"We are working under cover and we will be your house guests from now until New Year's. Those who love you from here and there lobbied to get you this one opportunity to pull your head out of your ass.

"Our job is to get you to see your life, your world and your future clearly rather than the crap covered lenses you usually look through. You are going to see your life has worth. As big a jerk as you are, you help folks despite your permanent wading pool full of self-pity you carry around with you every day like a damn badge of honor. We are going to help you find your better self. We know what you're feeling and thinking. We know everything about you."

"May I ask a question?" Nick asked.

"No, questions at the end," Cuthbert said.

"Let him ask a question," Bob said. "Go ahead, Nick?"

"Who the fuck are you guys, and you don't know jack shit about me," Nick said.

"That's your question?" Cuthbert said. "I thought you were going to ask me what kind of whisky I like. You're a detective, who do you think we are?"

"I think you are two lunatics about to be thrown out of my house" Nick said.

47

"You make a living as a detective...I'm surprised," Cuthbert said. He turned to Bob. "I'm going to have to tell him everything."

"I don't know if that's a good idea right now," Bob said.

"Now or never," Nick said.

Bob shrugged his shoulders. "Okay."

"Do you want the long answer or the short answer? I suggest the short answer so we can get to having a few drinks and making popcorn and watching the rest of *The Dark Knight*. So, long or short?"

"Short," Nick said.

"Good choice," Cuthbert said. "You asked who we are. This is Bob but you can call him Bobby boy."

"No, he can't," Bob protested.

"Yes, he can," Cuthbert said. "He is your guardian angel. He's been with you since you were six or something. I'm Cuthbert Quigle and I am a Christmas angel. I am also a very bad Christmas angel, but no one else wanted to deal with a dumb ass like you so they sent me.

"We are here because Bob was asked by your daughter and son, as well as Duke, Queenie and Tina to present your case to the Tribunal for a Divine Intervention. The Tribunal was made up of Peter, Michael and Gabriel. They decided that you were worth a try because of all the people who care about you, also pray for you. Even Baron sent a prayer."

Baron wagged his tail.

"There is concern that in forty or fifty years, if you continue on the path you are on, you will not be able to join your loved ones up there and you will have to pack a tank top and shorts and a fan for where you are going to end up.

"We are here to get you on the right path. Now you have free will and you can reject this opportunity, but we're here until New Year's," Cuthbert said. "If you reject us, we will just sit around and drink your booze, eat your food, smoke your cigars and play with your dogs. In our spare time we can help you shop for a portable air conditioner that will fit in your casket. We won't be around all the time. We have cover stories to explain why we're hanging around, so think of us as being undercover."

"Undercover?" Nick said.

"Do you need a dictionary to look up the words I'm using?"

"What are your cover stories? Nick asked.

"Bobby boy here is a former graduate student and knew you at Michigan. We will call him Robert Young; I used to love watching *Father knows Best* in the fifties. You of course may call him Bobby boy or if you prefer Bob. He is here in Chicago doing post grad research on criminal justice. He is a professor and associate dean at Ohio State," Cuthbert said.

Nick raised his eyebrow. "Ohio State?"

"I didn't say he was a particularly bright professor, and I did say he was an associate dean," Cuthbert said.

"And you," Nick asked, "what's your cover story?"

"I am a retired professor from Michigan, Cuthbert Quigle. I was one of your professors; in fact, I was your favorite professor. I have come to Chicago to relax and I have secured a position to support my trip at a mall where I will play Santa," Cuthbert said.

Nick laughed out loud. "Someone hired you to be Santa?"

"Don't laugh. I was hired because of my charm and my keen sense of humor," he said.

"So, you are angels, and I am supposed to call him Bobby boy and you're Cuthbert?"

"Since we are getting along so well, you may call me Cuth," he said.

"Okay, Cuth, and Bobby boy, prove to me that you are angels and not just two deranged con men," Nick said.

"What kind of proof do you want?" Bob asked.

"Tell me three things that I am the only one that knows," Nick said.

Bob said, "Okay, if you could, you would try to find a way to have a life with Maureen, the woman who's sister you shot and the woman who vowed to kill you for years."

"Nope, a lot of people I know believe that and you could have guessed it," Nick said. "You will have to do better than that."

"Let me try," Cuth said, "How about this, the brother of the Italian gentleman who has become a close friend of yours has a boat and named it 'Da Twins' after your sister Laura's children."

"There are a lot of people who know Joey's brother Antonio bought that boat," Nick said.

"Ah, but do they know that Antonio sent the two men who killed your two children to hell?" Cuth asked.

"Nick look surprised, "How did you know that?"

"I'm an angel, dumb ass," Cuth said. "Want more? How about this, you named your daughter after your older sister, Mary, who was born thirteen years before you. Billy was so tough on her she ran away when she was eighteen and you have been looking for her longer than you have been looking for your daughter's killers. Also, it's a family secret and in your immediate family, only your father, Wil, and you know. It has been kept from Phil and Laura and the other members of your family that may know but have never said a word. It has been a taboo subject with the Caldwells for almost forty years. How's that?"

Nick was silent, Baron and Ruby jumped on the couch and sat next to him. He looked like he was in shock.

Bob looked worried.

Cuthbert just kept looking at him. "Well?"

Nick looked up at Cuthbert. "The whisky is in the cabinet in the kitchen above the sink. The popcorn is in the pantry."

"Wonderful," Cuthbert said. "Can I make you a drink?"

Nick nodded. "Where do we go now?"

"We go to the Windy City and celebrate the holidays," Cuth said. "On the way back, you can explain to me why Blackie's closed."

Chapter 12

Nick and the rest of his merry band arrived back in Chicago late in the afternoon after stopping several times for Cuthbert to try different hamburgers on the way back.

Baron and Ruby immediately headed for the couch, Cuthbert and Bob sat down in the living room and Nick brought all the bags and boxes in from the cabin.

As he brought the last box in, he said with a little sarcasm, "Make yourselves at home."

Cuthbert said, "We have, we stayed here the night before last. I think you're going to have to get some fresh milk."

"Nick, I'm really sorry but we needed a place to stay and we thought we could get a better feel for you if we were surrounded by your things," Bob said.

"Yeah, I am personally impressed that you have open charges with so many pizza places," Cuthbert said.

"Nick, there are a few things we have to go over with you, so you don't get freaked out," Bob said.

"Too late, I am already freaked out and I am hoping that this is either a dream or a hallucination or a coma or a stroke, because if it isn't any of those things then I have already lost my mind and I should be checking if I am drooling on myself or have lost the ability to control my bladder," Nick said.

Cuth looked at him and said, "No, you're good, nothing on the sweater and you look dry."

Nick said, "Thank you."

"Your welcome," Cuth said. "So are you dreaming, hallucinating, in a coma, or stroking?"

Nick looked at him and said, "Too early to know."

"That's okay, we have a little more than two months to figure it out," Cuthbert said. "Hey, what were those cheesy things we had last night with the red pepper humus?"

"What cheesy things?" Nick asked.

"You know, they were sort of like potato chips?" Cuth asked.

"Doritos?" Nick asked.

"Yeah that's them, they were good, you need to get some more," Cuth said.

"I have a bag in a kitchen cabinet," Nick said.

"No, you don't, I ate them when we were watching movies here the other night," Cuth said. "Oh, and you probably need to get some more bourbon."

"Cuth, we really need to let Nick know what the parameters are in what we are doing. We've tried to pattern it after things that you are familiar with, so that we can find a synergy between all parties," Bob said.

"I told you he was an inflated asshole," Cuth said.

"Nick, I never said that you were an inflated asshole," Bob said.

"I wasn't talking to you, Bobby boy," Cuth said.

Nick laughed. "Bob, I think you that you are trying to establish a pattern that is familiar for me to help enhance interaction, cooperation and collaboration so that we can accomplish whatever goal you believe you have to achieve here. But did you taken into consideration that having two angels drop in to spend the holidays because my children and pups who are now in heaven went to a tribunal made up of two archangels and the top apostle and the gatekeeper to heaven to plead for an intervention so I can be admitted into heaven for any semi-rational person would be a lot to swallow? And on top of that, said angels will be house guests that appear that they are planning on eating and drinking me out of house and home. The bonus is to plan to follow me around and mix in with my family and friends. Now I appreciate you have a job to do, but I reserve the right to be creeped out and a little apprehensive."

"He's got a point," Cuth said.

"Stay out of this," Bob said. "Nick, I just want you to know there is really nothing to worry about."

"You mean other than not conforming in the way you wish and being condemned to everlasting suffering in hell?" Nick said.

"Hey, who said we would send you to California or Portland?" Cuth said.

"Cuth, please," Bob said. "Some of your concerns I can address by briefing you on the protocol for this type of intervention."

"Translation, Nick, here are the instructions that will give you a fighting chance not to be sent to Seattle or someplace like that, but you might do okay, you do live in Chicago with Mayor Lighthead," Cuth said.

"Foot," Nick said, "Lightfoot."

"I knew it was something like that," Cuth said. "Give him the damn details so we can eat and watch the movie."

Bob cleared his throat. "Nick, what I meant was you like film, so much of this is based on those types of references."

"I get it, I'm your Scrooge, so am I more like George C. Scott, Reginald Owen, Alastair Sim or Albert Finney?"" Nick asked.

"Bill Murray or Scrooge McDuck has my vote," Cuth said.

"So, which of you is the angel of Christmas past and Christmas present and future?" Nick asked.

"It's not like that," Bob said.

"Yeah, Cuthbert said, "we're more like Dudley in the *Bishop's Wife* or Clarence with an edge in *"It's a Wonderful Life."*

"That is the weirdest thing I have heard in a long time," Nick said.

"It is but he's not that far off," Bob said

"If you think that's weird, listen to this. You remember the Christmas song about Rudolf?" Cuth asked. "But do you know what really happened?"

"I'm sure you're going to tell me," Nick said.

You know how it goes, all of the other reindeer used to laugh and call him names. They never let poor Rudolph join in any reindeer games. Then one foggy Christmas Eve..." Cuthbert asked

"Yeah I remember."

"This is right up your alley, Nick. Do you know those reindeer were pretty crappy to Red. Do you know what happened on that foggy Christmas Eve, Nick?" Cuth asked

"What," Nick asked.

Cuthbert continued, "Well, Nick, Rudolph killed them, he killed all of them, every last one of those motherf..."

"CUTHBERT," Bob yelled, "enough!"

Nick and Cuthbert both burst into laughter while Bob turned the shade of Satan.

"Can you two just shut the..." Bob was interrupted by Cuthbert.

"Bob, don't say it, it will take more than a bell to get your wings back."

"May I please just finish?" Bob asked.

Nick nodded.

"There aren't that many rules, the first is everyone you know will be able to see us, just like in the movies. Rule two, you can't tell them we are angels or why we are here."

"What do you mean, I can't?" Nick asked.

"You remember David Niven in *The Bishop's Wife*? That will be you," Bob said.

"I can't tell anyone?" Nick asked.

"No, you can't," Bob said, "and on the stroke of midnight on New Year's, you and every person that we will come in contact with won't remember Cuthbert and I were ever here."

"Tell him about the loophole," Cuth said.

"Really," Bob said.

"If you don't, I will," Cuth said.

"Go ahead, tell him," Bob said.

55

"Nick, while we're with you, you will be able to talk to and understand any dog or cat or squirrel or frog, any animal. And while we are here you can communicate with any animal here or that has crossed over the bridge," Cuth said. "But at Midnight on New Year's Day, those conversations will be remembered but as dreams... cool, huh?"

Nick looked at them and poured three fingers of Jameson's in a glass and drank it down like it was a glass of water.

Cuthbert turned to Bob and said, "I think that went well, don't you?"

The look Bob gave Cuthbert was like the look Peter gave those at the gate that would be directed to the down elevator.

Chapter 13

The next morning Nick said, "Do you have a plan how I explain two people that my family and friends have never heard of will be hanging around and staying at my house through New Year's?"

"Yes," Cuthbert said. "Bob and I keep in contact; I have always felt sorry for my witless students. Bob interviewed Ronnie Silk and Mo Jones about criminal law. He 'discovered,'"--Cuthbert gave air quotes with a breakfast burrito in one hand, as Baron and Ruby were hopeful it would fall—"get this, that you all know each other, and Bob called me and said wouldn't it be fun if we went to Chicago and reacquainted ourselves with our old buddy, Nick Caldwell. We could even get all those keen novels that have been written about him, autographed. So, what do you think?"

"They are detectives, they are going to think you're crazy," Nick said.

"Probably not," Bob said.

"Of course they will. They're not going to buy that," Nick said.

"Nick, the truth is," Cuthbert said, "since you did your disappearing act and took off to the great white north with the pups and didn't take a cell, didn't check in with them, and you walked out on them, they have been trying to find you. Actually, Nicholas," Cuth almost sounded like Mrs. Marbulls, "they are worried, scared and angry and they believe that you have had a breakdown. No, Nick, they are going to be so relieved that you are okay and so pissed off at you, they will hardly notice us."

"And they will be happy that two old friends showed up to be with you over the holidays, so you're not on your own," Bob said. "They will invite us to the holiday festivities, they will confide in us and they will see and will think it is a good thing that you are connecting with two old friends."

"Particularly," Cuthbert said, "if one of those old friends is a jolly old elf, HO...HO...HO."

Nick looked at him and said, "You two would make great criminals."

Cuthbert blushed, as he was chugging his morning mimosa.

"How do you do that in the morning?" Nick asked.

Cuth smiled, "We can't get drunk."

"Okay, so what's the plan?" Nick asked.

"We plan to drop in on you and surprise you in front of your staff," Bob said. "Then you will introduce us and that will be that."

"And then of course you will take us out to lunch, and there you will invite us to stay at your house, because we have so much to reminisce and catch up about," Cuthbert said. "We could go to the Village and meet Joey the Bat and Antonio; we may not get a chance we meet them when we leave here." Cuth made a sad face and pointed down.

Nick shook his head, called Baron and Ruby and walked out the door.

Chapter 14

As Nick walked up the stairs to the office with Baron and Ruby, he could hear the voices and the sounds of a busy office; people on the phone, the copy machine and the people moving around. When he got to the top of the steps and walked through the door, the rooms fell silent. Everyone in the front office stopped what they were doing and just stared. Baron and Ruby walked over to Katie and sat on either side of her and adopted the same disapproving look. Constance, now fully recovered, stood the door of her office. Phil stood by Mrs. Marbulls' desk, and both looked angry. It was Monday, the day of the weekly staff meeting. Greg and Felix were walking up the front steps, having come over from conferring with the other lab at the Wabash office. They stopped at the door and just looked at Nick.

Nick didn't see Bart, and thought maybe he was late for the meeting, then heard him say, "What the hell is going on?" as he walked out of his office. He stopped in his tracks, looked at Nick and said, "Could we have a word in my office, please."

"Sure, hello everyone," Nick said. No one answered.

Nick walked in and Bart closed the door. "Have a seat."

Nick sat, and said, "First of all I want to..."

He was interrupted by a slow, calm and firm voice from a man that was turning the shade of the Chicago Bulls road uniforms or the shade of a matador's cape. Bart asked, "Could you please tell me if you are fucking-out-of-your-mind?"

"Why, yes I am," Nick said, "and thank you for asking."

Bart said, "Not funny."

"A little funny," Nick said.

"No, it's not," Bart said. "The last we talked, you were going to Detroit to see Ronnie and Mo about a case."

"I cancelled," Nick said, "and then I thought about going on my way back."

"Back from where?" Bart asked.

"I took the pups and went to northern Michigan," Nick said. Both Ruby and Baron had a look on their face like they didn't want to be included in the conversation.

"Why?" Bart asked.

"To chill, to process, to decompress," Nick said.

"You do remember that I used to be a shrink, so cut the psycho babel," Bart said.

"After the Crowe thing, I needed to get out of here," Nick said.

"I understand that, but I don't understand why you didn't tell someone that, let them know you were okay, send a damn postcard. Those people out there were worried, all of them. Your brother called Laura and Bob in St. Louis. Casey and Alex called here weekly. Sinclair offered to come and 'look for your sorry ass. There was a call from an unidentified woman."

Bart and Nick said in unison, "Maureen."

"Constance and Phil looked all over Chicago for you and Wil called every day. Your father called Dalton and Sinclair and said he was worried. Sinclair told him it was exactly like you because you are a world class asshole sometimes. Felix and Greg took turns going to the city morgue looking for John Doe's."

"They weren't looking for me, they like going there, like some people like going to amusement parks," Nick said.

"Still not funny," Bart said.

"Katie cried and went over to Billy's every night to sit with him, Alana tried to get Cal Simon and Wil to open up a missing person investigation and Mrs. Marbulls," Bart's voiced trailed off.

"I'm dead aren't I," Nick said, without a doubt.

"I'd say pretty much. Here is what I think you need to do; you need to go into your office and sit behind your desk and say something that isn't lame to each one of these people. They were worried and now they are hurt," Bart said.

"Are you shrinking me?" Nick asked.

"It's what I need to do sometimes. You also at some point need to tell me what is really going on," Bart said.

"I think I'm losing it," Nick said.

"I'm pretty sure you're losing it," Bart said.

"I'm not kidding," Nick said.

"Neither am I," Bart replied.

"You understand, I have two A...that are following me around and will until New Year's," Nick Said.

"You have two A's following you?"

"No, two A..., following me.

"Two whats?..., Aardvarks? Alligators? Albatrosses? Two Alpacas?" Bart asked.

"Oh my God, it's true," Nick said.

"Let me get this straight," Bart said, "you have two A's following you?"

"What they said was true," Nick said.

"Who said, the Aardvark? The Alpaca? Who said?"

Nick looked discouraged. "Never mind."

"You know maybe today wouldn't be a good day to talk to the staff," Bart said. "Why don't you wait until tomorrow, I'll explain to everyone that you want to meet with them individually tomorrow."

Mrs. Marbulls' voice came over the intercom, "There are two gentlemen, who are friends from his college days, here to see Mr. Caldwell."

"He'll be right out," Bart said.

"That's them," Nick said.

Bart peaked out the door. "I don't think so, neither of them look like an Aardvark or an Alpaca. One looks like a nerd and the other...," Bart smiled, "looks like Santa Claus."

Chapter 15

Nick walked out of his office and Bob was sitting in a chair in deep conversation with Constance. He overheard Bob say, "I was so sorry that you were injured recently."

"How did you know about that?" she asked.

"Nick was very concerned about you," he said.

Nick turned around when he heard loud laughter. It was Mrs. Marbulls, who was laughing so loud he thought she might start snorting. Cuthbert was sitting on her desk telling her a story...HE WAS SITTING ON HER DESK! And there was no sign that she intended to shoot him.

It was now official. Nick had crossed over to the *Twilight Zone* or *Superman's Bizarro World.* There were unnatural things afoot.

Cuthbert turned to Nick and smiled.

It was now a confirmed fact. Nick believed he had officially lost all his marbles, or he was dreaming, or he was dead and had been sent to hell with a nerd and Santa as escorts.

"Oh, Nick," Cuthbert said, "We thought we would drop by and see where it all happened. You work with wonderful people?"

"Professor, would you and Bob like to see my office?" Nick had no idea why he said what he had just said.

"Delighted," Cuthbert said, in a robust and irritating Santa way. "Bob, Nick wants to show us his office."

"Wonderful, I've never seen a real big-time gumshoe's office," Bob said with a 1960's -1970's *Up with People* glazed smile on his face.

"Come on in guys. We have some catching up to do," Nick said, mimicking Bob's tone.

They followed Nick into his office. Nick shut the door. Baron and Ruby sat almost at attention on the couch.

"May I ask exactly what the hell do you think you are doing?" Nick asked.

"We're getting to know you and those you care about better," Bob said.

"That Mrs. Marbles is a stitch, what a wonderful and cheerful woman," Cuthbert said.

Baron and Ruby looked at Cuthbert and wagged their tails. Nick glared at them.

"Come on, Nick, lighten up a little, you need to smile sometimes," Cuthbert said.

"He's right, you need to laugh and enjoy life a little," Bob said.

"Hey, I know you see a lot of bad things in your line of work, but that doesn't have to define you," Cuthbert said. "It could be worse; you could be a...I don't know teach at a university."

"Or worse, be an administrator at a college," Bob said.

"I don't think he could do that, Bob," Cuthbert said. "Nick has a sense of right and wrong and he has the courage of his convictions."

"Yeah, I guess you're right. I apologize, Nick, I didn't mean it as an insult," Bob said.

"I didn't take it as an insult. I know some good college administrators," Nick said.

Cuthbert and Bob looked at each other, then looked at Baron and Ruby, and all four of them burst into laughter.

"Okay, that's enough," Nick said. "What specifically are you doing here?"

"Do you mean here, here today or here in general?" Cuthbert asked, "because you know why we are here in general."

Bob spoke: "We are here in general at the request of your children and the pups who have loved you over your life. We are going to try to get you back to the person who was happy and could see the good in the world. The person who could love and understand that it is okay to love. You love the people you work with; you love your family; you have friends, and you have people who care for you, but you rarely

63

acknowledge it. It isn't enough to care and love, you need to express it."

"Thank you, Dr. Phil," Nick said.

Cuthbert laughed out loud. "He is a smartass, but I like him."

Baron and Ruby smiled and wagged their tails.

"What do you want from me?" Nick asked.

"We want you not to just be alive and exist in this world," Cuthbert said.

Bob continued, "We want you to live, really live and enjoy this world."

"Wonderful," Nick said, with more than a hint of sarcasm. "What's next, will I be visited by three spirits?"

"Three, you already have two," Cuthbert said.

Bob sighed, "Cuth, that was a literary reference."

"I knew that," Cuthbert said. "Nick, you do realize that Dicken's wrote fiction, right?"

Nick looked at him with no expression.

Cuthbert looked around Nick's office and said, "Perhaps, I asked the wrong question."

"What do you think the right question would be?" Bob asked.

"Maybe I should have asked," Cuthbert said, "you do realize that Dashiell Hammett wrote fiction?"

Cuthbert, Bob and the pups laughed again. Nick did not.

"Look at the time," Cuthbert said. "I'm famished, let's go and get something to eat. Let's go to the Eleven City Diner, I heard they have a wonderful brisket."

Bob said, "That sounds wonderful."

Cuthbert looked at Nick. "Okay with you?"

Nick just looked at him.

"Oh, come on, Nick, you can't mourn the closing of Blackie's forever. Besides, they have great deserts at Eleven," Cuthbert said. "You're going to need your strength because this evening we start your work."

"My work?" Nick said.

"Your work," Bob said.

"What exactly is my work?" Nick said.

Bob answered, "Transforming you into the half full guy that you are deep down…"

Cuthbert interrupted, "Way, way deep down"

"Instead of the empty guy you have let yourself believe you are," Bob continued.

"You mean half empty, like the half full, half empty glass reference," Nick said.

"No, Nick. He means almost empty. If you were a car, soon we'd be pushing you into a gas station," Cuthbert said.

"If I rang a bell would you two just go away?" Nick asked.

"Ahh, a film reference, Capra, very good. No, we wouldn't go away," Cuthbert said. "May I ask you a question?"

"Sure, why not," Nick said.

Cuthbert smiled, "Are you familiar with any films that have been made in this century or any films that are not in black and white?"

Nick got up from his desk, walked over to the coat rack, got his coat and said, "Come on, let's go eat."

Cuthbert gave his thunderous Santa laugh and said, "Wonderful!"

Chapter 16

That evening after dinner they sat around the fire: Baron, Ruby and Nick on the couch, Bob in a chair across from Nick, and Cuthbert in Nick's Lazy Boy.

"What is the point of all this?" Nick asked.

"Let me try to explain this to you in a way you can understand," Cuthbert said. "Our mission is to turn you away from your Mr. Potter tendencies and…"

"And make me into George Bailey?" Nick said, mockingly.

"No, certainly not," Cuthbert said. "We want you to see the world and your life from the perspective of Zuzu. We want you to see the magic and the belief in life, your life. We want to help you restore a child's wonder and happiness that you once had a long time ago. So, shut up and focus."

"I don't like this, and I don't see how it will help or even what it is supposed to accomplish." Nick said.

"You're not supposed to like it," Cuth said.

"Honest self-introspection isn't pleasant; no one enjoys looking back. You're going to look at the good, the bad and the ugly," Bob said.

"Film reference," Cuth said with glee.

Bob and Nick looked at him.

"Okay, I just thought things needed to lighten up a bit," Cuth said. "After all, you're a lawyer."

"I am not a lawyer," Nick said. "I am a private investigator."

"With a law degree and an active Bar membership," Cuth said.

"Granted, but I don't practice, and I don't want to practice," Nick said.

"Why don't you practice, you're already that good at it?" Cuth joked.

"No, I just don't do that kind of work," Nick said.

"Why, you could do some good for folks, maybe, people who can't get good legal help," Bob said. "Things are going so well with the firm, Bart has it covered, so you can do anything you want to do."

"Bob surprisingly makes a good point," Cuth said.

"I just don't want to be responsible to people in that way. I'd like to drop this now," Nick said.

"Okay, sue me," Cuth said. "Hey, you actually could sue me," Cuth laughed.

Nick did not see the humor.

Bob said, "Fine we'll cover this later."

"I don't think so," Nick growled.

"We think we will," Cuth said.

"What do you want from me?" Nick asked.

"Honesty," Bob said, "you have avoided dealing with a lot of things in your life. We want you to deal with them so you can move forward."

"You know you are beginning to sound like a Dr. Phil," Nick said.

"I wish, do you know how much Dr. Phil makes?" Cuth asked.

Thoroughly irritated, Nick said, "NO."

"Oh...neither do I, but I bet it's a lot," Cuth said.

"Really?" Nick said.

"Really," Cuth said, totally missing Nick's point.

"Fine, the quicker we get done with you, the quicker you can leave," Nick said.

"Leave? We're not leaving until the holidays are over. We are your Christmas Buddies," Cuth said, with a big smile. Baron jumped up on Cuth's lap.

"Traitor," Nick said to Baron. Baron wagged his tail. "What about you, Ruby?"

Ruby walked over to Nick and licked his hand, then walked over to Cuth and sat by his chair.

"I'm surrounded by traitors," Nick said.

"No, you're surrounded by those who care about you," Bob said.

"And I promised them bacon strips, biscuits and a muffin," Cuth said.

Chapter 17

It was getting light out when they stopped talking. The last eight hours seemed like days. It reminded Nick of an early show that for some unexplained reason, Billy, Nick's dad, had bought the "ultimate collection" on Amazon, of *This is Your Life* starring Ralph Edwards. Old Ralph would ambush some celebrity and invade their privacy by delving into their lives before they became famous. Nick was looking out the window and was wondering and thinking about why his dad would buy a show like that.

Cuth said, "Because he loved your mother and they would watch it together, so when he is alone at home now, since none of his sons drop by to see him much, he sits alone in his chair, the one next to the chair that was your mother's, and he watches the show and talks to her because he misses her. That's why your father bought that collection. He also bought the Jack Benny Show and *You Bet Your Life* with Groucho Marx."

"I didn't know that," Nick said.

"It's private," Bob said, "he's mourning."

"Yeah, you ought to try it," Cuth said.

"I've mourned," Nick said.

"No, you haven't," Cuth said, as he scarfed down a pop tart.

"What do you know about it? I've mourned for my children," Nick said.

"You haven't mourned; you've been angry," Cuth said. "You've wanted vengeance; you wanted to punish the people who did it. You were more than willing to let Antonio do the dirty work for you. You don't know how to mourn, but you do know how to get even; you're just not very good at it. What you are good at is wallowing in self-pity."

"The men responsible for my children's deaths are in prison," Nick said.

"Very good, Nick," Cuth said.

"Cuth, don't," Bob said.

"No, Bob, this self-righteous jerk needs to hear the truth," Cuth said. "That was very good, Nick. 'The men responsible for my children's deaths are in prison.' Are you sure that you don't want to practice law? You talk like a lawyer. Just the facts, no emotion, just the cold-hard facts."

"I don't need this," Nick exploded.

"Good, Nick, you have all the emotions from A to A, anger to more anger," Cuth said.

"Just drop it," Nick said.

"We can't do that, Nick, and I think you know that," Bob said.

"Have you ever talked about your loss?" Cuth asked.

"Of course, I have," Nick said. "I gave a statement, and I discussed the crime scene..."

"That's not what I mean. Have you ever spoken to anyone about how you felt? How hurt you are? How you cry every night," Cuth said.

"I don't cry," Nick said.

"Oh, that must have been Baron or Ruby we heard last night," Cuth said.

"Nick, I'm your guardian, and I know what you do each night. I know how Baron and now Ruby curl up around you so that you can feel you aren't alone and you're not," Bob said.

"You don't have to play the tough guy. We know it's horse puckey," Cuth said.

"Horse puckey?" Bob asked.

"I heard it in a TV show once... TV reference," Cuth said. "And stop the getting shot thing. I have heard of criminals trying to commit suicide by cop, but this suicide by bad guy thing you've got going isn't going to work. All it does is make extra work for Bob and runs up your insurance premiums, waste of time."

"You're going to see them again," Bob said.

"But on the 'Big Guy's' schedule, not yours," Cuth added.

70

"I didn't try to commit suicide," Nick said, with little conviction.

"Didn't you learn before your first confession in first grade, it's bad to lie?" Cuth asked. "When Charlotte tried to shoot you, you hesitated, you gave her the first shot, almost got Reverend Lizzy killed, and if it weren't for Duke, you would have let that Crowe kid finish you off. What about the sniper that went after Antonio's boys, you tried to draw his fire. You were lucky that time. By the way, they say 'hello.' St. Louis was the best. You put yourself out there as bait when you knew the killer was following you. You took more chances than Charles Bronson took in the first *Death Wish*...." Cuth turned to Bob and smiled.

"I know, film reference," Bob said.

"You bet your halo," Cuth said. "Nick, you didn't even come clean with that priest friend of yours and we know about that other thing too, but we'll take that up at another time."

"We probably should let Nick get some sleep," Bob said.

"Yeah, you're right and I need a drink," Cuth said, heading towards the liquor cabinet.

"It's six o'clock in the morning," Nick said.

"It's okay, I'm not on central standard time," Cuth said. "I will see you in a few hours at brunch."

"Brunch?" Nick said.

"Yeah, great invention, a meal between breakfast and lunch," Cuth said. "After brunch I have to get down to the store and get measured for my new St. Nick's suit, not to be confused with a Nick in denial suit. Hey, I have a great idea, you and Bob can join me for lunch at the mall around one. We can talk about dinner plans later. I'm thinking maybe the Village, and you could invite Joey and Antonio...who knows, maybe joey can ask Santa for a Louisville slugger."

Nick started to head to his room, then he turned to Cuth and asked, "May I ask you a question?"

"Absolutely," Cuth said.

71

"How did you get into heaven?" Nick asked.

"It was *Sweet Charity*," Cuth said and turned to Bob, "film and theatre reference, double points."

Bob nodded.

"I'm serious," Nick said.

"Charm and I'm *Simply Irresistible*," Cuth said. "*Carry on My Wayward Son.*"

"I know, two music references," Bob said.

"And a TV reference too; they play the song Kansas on *Supernatural* all the time...double points."

"I wouldn't say all the time, not every show," Bob said.

"But enough," Cuth countered.

The angels continued to kibitz over the points to be awarded in this weird contest that they were participating in. They didn't even notice that Nick and the pups went to bed.

Chapter 18

Bart entered Nick's office and looked at him slumped over with his head on his desk, "Partying with St. Nick too much for you?"

Nick groaned.

"You sound like crap," Bart said.

Another groan.

"You look like crap," Bart said. He looked over on the couch and Ruby and Baron were both lying on the couch with their legs in the air, snoring. "What did you do to your dogs?"

"Nothing," Nick said. "This is the general condition you end up in if you spend any time around Cuthbert. He will either talk you to death or drink you to death or sleep deprive you to death."

"Well, which one is it this morning?" Bart asked.

"A little of all three," Nick grunted out. "First, he talks at you until you need a drink, then he keeps giving you drinks until you want to pass out or want to sleep, then he doesn't let you sleep or pass out. He just continues talking."

"Sounds like the house guest from hell," Bart said.

"Not hell," Nick said. "Hell would be good; you would expect the torture in hell."

"So how long are they staying?" Bart asked.

"It doesn't matter, it's going to seem like an eternity," Nick said.

"He called this morning," Bart said.

"What? Why? He called you?" Nick said.

"He did," Bart replied.

"What the hell did he want?"

"He wanted to know about your sister," Bart said.

"Laura, why would he ask about her?" Nick asked.

"Not Laura, the other one," Bart said.

Nick was fully awake now, "What did you say?"

"I told him I didn't know what he was talking about," Bart said.

"What did he say," Nick asked.

"He said it was a naughty thing to tell a fib to Santa during the Christmas season," Bart said.

"Then what?" Nick asked. "What did he want to know?"

"I asserted that I did not know what he was talking about," Bart said. "Then he said that he had to go to work and that I should go into my right desk drawer and get your sister's phone number out of the file and give it to him. Then he reminded me it was the same drawer I keep Mary's & little William's file in and the files on the Crowes and the sensitive files on the Carrandinis, the one that has two key locks and one combination lock."

"What happened then?" Nick asked.

"I'm sorry Nick, but I went into the drawer and gave him her name, phone, address and work information. Nick, how in the hell did he know. How did he know where it was kept?" Bart asked.

"He knows because he is an A..., A..., Uhn..., screw it," Nick said.

"Because he's an asshole?" Bart said.

"That too," Nick said.

"Why does he want that information?" Bart asked.

Nick replied, "Heaven knows, literally."

"Nick, I don't know why I gave him the information. I told him no twice, then I felt compelled to give it to him. I didn't want to, but I did," Bart said.

"I know, I felt the same way last night when he was talking to me," Nick said.

"What are you going to do about this?" Bart asked.

"Well, I'm going to the mall," Nick said.

"You're going to a mall?" Bart said.

"Yeah, I'm going to see Santa and give him my Christmas list, then I'm going to tell him where he can stuff it," Nick said.

At that comment, Baron and Ruby rolled over and sat up on the couch. Nick thought he saw both Baron and Ruby shaking their heads "no," but thought he was just imagining it. Baron hopped down and stood in front of the door. He looked worried. Ruby stood on the couch with a worried look on her face and whined.

"What's up with you two?" Nick said. "Go back and lie down. I'll be back soon."

Baron slowly walked back to the couch and hopped back up. They both sat down with a worried look and they both whimpered a little.

"Hey, what are you worrying about?" Nick said.

"Maybe they are worried about you confronting Santa," Bart said.

"First of all, he is not Santa, he is Cuthbert, apparently an eternal pain in the ass. I will strongly suggest that I do not want him staying at my house over the holidays and that he needs to leave and delving into my private family business is inappropriate," Nick said. "What can he do?'

Nick walked out of the office with Bart.

Baron turned to Ruby. "What can he do? He could get Nick sent to everlasting suffering in hell!"

"Really," Ruby said. "Does that mean we should get Nick beach wear for Christmas?"

Baron gave Ruby a serious look with just a hint of disgust. "Not Funny."

"Oh, it was funny," she replied.

"No, it wasn't," Baron said.

This conversation continued for at least an hour, devolving into a rather academic and esoteric discussion into what was funny, what was comedic and finally the relationship between comedy and satire.

All those classes at obedience school were not wasted. They really did set a new tone for their conversations. Continuing education is essential to developing a well-rounded hound.

Chapter 19

As Nick walked through the large suburban mall, he looked at the all the Christmas decorations in place. It was the eve before Thanksgiving, the forgotten holiday, his father, Billy, would always say. The lights were lit, and Santa Village was open for business. You could have your picture taken with Santa, order as many copies as you could afford, and you could have the picture printed on t-shirts, sweatshirts, cups, plaques, even a towel.

Cuthbert said early this morning, "If you had enough money, you could probably have your Santa picture laser printed on your ass... in color." Nick wondered if Billy would like something like that for Christmas. Probably not.

Former Chicago P.D. Detective and Deputy Chief William "Billy" Caldwell Sr. was a Christmas purist, complete with a life-size nativity scene on half of the front lawn and an homage to Santa on the other side. But the display had not been put up yet. In fact, there were no decorations outside or inside, nor would there be any Christmas music played at the senior Caldwell's home until after the turkey was eaten and the pumpkin pie was finished at Thanksgiving dinner. Then, decorating would commence and continue all day Friday. Christmas didn't begin until after Thanksgiving.

Nick shuttered a little when he thought about joining his family for Thanksgiving. His sister, Laura, asked and shamed him into coming. She and her husband and their twins would be there as well as her other brothers, Phil, and his girlfriend of the month, as well as, Wil and his fiancé. Of course, Bart and Jonathon would attend and Katie and Greg, known as Nick's wards, would also be there. Even though Nick loved these people, he always dreaded the holidays since he had lost his children and to add insult to injury this year, he would have to bring with him Cuthbert and Bob his houseguest A...un...gel...s, screw it.

As he got closer to Santa Village, he could see Cuthbert in costume on his throne with a line of children waiting to see him. Nick noticed instead of the salt n' pepper grey hair, Cuthbert's hair and beard were white as snow. It wasn't a wig or a false beard either. Apparently, A...un..g..., screw it, those spirit types with wings can change their hair color at will.

Nick saw Bob standing at the side of Santa Village, probably trying to keep an eye on Cuthbert. Nick walked over to where Bob was standing. "Has he done much damage to the psychological well-being of any of the children yet?"

Bob replied, "Not yet, but it is only a matter of time."

Nick and Bob listened to Cuthbert work his "magic."

In this politically correct world, children do not sit on Santa's lap anymore; they sit beside Santa on a bench. A little girl approached Santa and sat down.

Cuthbert gave out an unenthusiastic, "Ho, Ho, Ho."

"Hi, Santa," the little girl said.

"Yeah, what's your name?" Cuthbert said.

"Mandy," she said.

"Are your parents Barry Manilow fans?" he asked.

Mandy looked confused.

"Never mind. You been good, kid?"

"I have been good, Santa," she replied.

"So, what do you want for Christmas?" Cuthbert said.

"I want world peace," the little princess said.

"Are you running for Miss America, kid?" he asked.

"No, Santa," she said.

"You should," he replied, "is there any gift you would like for yourself?"

Nick and Bob cringed a little.

"Yes, Santa, I would like a mermaid tail blanket," she said.

"A mermaid tail blanket? Really?" he said.

"Really, Santa," she said.

"Okay, good to know, I'll see what I can do."

"Thank you, Santa," she said, sweetly.

"No problem, kid, and think about that Miss America thing," he said. "Next."

Bob and Nick looked at each other.

"Wasn't that bad," Bob said.

"Yeah," Nick said.

A little boy made his way up to Santa's perch, looking a little scared. Cuthbert noticed this and said, "Don't be afraid, son, I'm Santa, not a hellhound."

Bob and Nick cringed and just shook their heads.

The little guy didn't seem comforted.

"What's your name?" he said.

"Tommy," the little guy replied.

"Well, Tommy, what would you like for Christmas?" Cuthbert asked.

"I'd like a pony," Tommy said.

Cuthbert looked a little surprised. "You want a pony?"

"Yes, Santa,' Tommy said.

"Where do you live, Tommy?" Cuthbert said.

"We live in a tall building in the Loop," Tommy said.

"Where would you keep the pony?" Cuthbert asked.

"In my room," Tommy answered.

"Listen, Tommy, if you are good...pony. If you're bad, dead pony," he said and he laughed,

Tommy and his mother did not laugh.

One of the store managers rushed up to Santa's throne and said, "Santa needs to take a break and go to lunch; he'll be back in a little while."

"Cool," Santa said.

A very angry and red-faced manger turned to him and said, "Are you crazy, what were you doing up there? We need to have a talk. How could you do something like that?"

Cuthbert looked at the manager directly in the eye and said very quietly, "Do you think we really need to talk?"

The manager said "I...I...I think..., no, I guess we don't."

"Do you really think I am crazy?" Cuthbert asked him.

The manager said, "Well, maybe we should..."

78

Cuthbert continued to stare into his eyes.

"No, I don't," the manager said.

Cuthbert said, "I think I need to go to lunch, don't you?"

"I do," said the manager. "Yes, you should go to lunch."

"Okay, I will," Cuthbert said with a big Santa smile. "I guess you need to go back to your office and get some work done but thank you for coming up here to check on me."

"I do," said the manager. "It's always a pleasure to talk with you."

"I know," Cuthbert said. They both smiled.

"I'm going back to my office, have a good lunch," the manager said.

"Thank you, I will," Cuthbert said and walked over to Bob and Nick.

Bob said, "Cuthbert, you know that you should not do what you did."

"What did I do?" Cuth said.

"You know what you did," Bob said.

Cuthbert smiled, "I just used my natural charm."

Nick interrupted. "Come on, Bob, let's go to lunch with Rasputin here."

Cuthbert smiled and strolled toward the food court.

Chapter 20

As Nick, Bob and the "anti-Santa" walked to the food court none of them said anything. They walked into one of the small restaurants and sat. The server came over and took their drink order. As she walked away, Nick and Bob just stared at Cuthbert.

"What?" Cuthbert asked.

"What," Bob said. "What do you think you were doing? Why did you feel it was necessary to traumatize that little boy?"

"Oh, come on, he wanted a pony and he thought he could keep it in his bedroom in a Loop condo. Somebody had to wise him up, "Cuthbert said.

"And you're the guy to do that?" Nick asked.

"If not Santa, who?" Cuthbert laughed.

Bob asked, "What about little Mandy?"

"What about Mandy?" Cuthbert said.

"All she said was that she wanted world peace and you mocked her," Nick said.

"Then you pulled that Vulcan mind meld on the mall manager. You're not supposed to do stuff like that," Bob said. "Have you heard the term low profile?"

The server returned with their drinks and took the food order. They sat in silence for a few moments.

"What is the big deal?" Cuthbert said. "No harm, no foul."

"You don't know that," Nick said. "You may have ruined those kids' Christmas."

"You think Christmas is about ponies and mermaid blankets?" Cuthbert asked.

"It is for them at this age," Nick said.

"Those kids believe in Santa and Christmas, they believe in the spirit of Christmas," Bob said. "At that age is when they start practicing and developing their beliefs. There is no harm in that, let them have their childhood."

"You guys are making a big deal about nothing," Cuthbert said.

"Christmas isn't nothing to little kids like that. It's something they look forward to all year," Bob said.

Bob's cell phone rang.

"I didn't know you all had cell phones," Nick said.

"When in Rome..." Cuthbert said.

"Where's yours?" Nick asked.

"They didn't give me one," Cuthbert said. "Some of them up there have trust issues."

"You mean they have trust issues with you," Nick said.

Bob answered, "Yes sir, he is right here." He listened and at one point moved the phone away from his ear, then said, "It's for you," and handed the phone to Cuthbert.

"Hello, who am I speaking to?" he said. He too had to move the phone away from his ear. "I better take this in private." Cuthbert got up and walked into a nook near the restrooms to talk.

Cuthbert began to speak, "How good of you to..."

The voice on the other end said, "Shut your cookie hole and listen to me very carefully."

"Yes sir," Cuthbert said.

"What in the name of the Yule Tide do you think you were doing?" the voice said.

"Well, Kris, I thought it would be appropriate to wise them up to the true meaning of the holiday..." Cuthbert said.

"You think that was appropriate?" Kris asked.

"Well," Cuthbert said.

"Well nothing," Kris said. "That's not your job, you got that?"

"But sir, I was..." Cuthbert was interrupted.

"You were being a jerk," Kris said. "Listen to me, if you continue the way you are going, you will not only have your dwelling when you return full of coal, but I will get you transferred and you will be mucking the reindeer's stalls for the next two hundred years, you got that?"

"Yes, sir," Cuthbert said.

"You are lucky, Cuthbert, that I don't have Comet and Prancer do a holiday tap dance on your head and Dasher and Blitzen tap dance on your behind until it is as red as Rudolph's nose...are we clear?"

"We are, sir," Cuthbert said.

"We had better be. Don't mess with my brand again, do we understand each other?" Kris demanded.

"We do, sir," Cuthbert said.

"And put a little more enthusiasm into those, Ho, Ho, Ho's; the kids expect it. You sound like Cupid when he's constipated. Straighten up or you'll find a rake with your name on it. Cuthbert, you've been very, very naughty." Kris hung up.

Cuthbert walked back to the restaurant and sat down.

"Everything okay?" Nick asked

"Perfect," Cuthbert said, without much enthusiasm.

"So?" Bob asked.

"Kris just wanted to give me a few tips about the job," Cuthbert said.

"I bet he did," Bob said. "Nick, I'm pretty sure our friend here will not be wanting for material to burn in his stove this year."

"I hope he told you to work on those, Ho, Ho, Ho's; you kind of sound like Baron and Ruby when they have gas," Nick said.

"You two would be great in a Christmas Pageant, you could play the donkey. I just don't know who the better backend would be," Cuthbert said.

"Ouch," said Nick.

"Let's talk about tomorrow and Thanksgiving," Cuthbert said.

"Cuthbert, we haven't been invited," Bob said.

"Bob's invited," Nick said.

"I'm not invited?" Cuthbert asked indignantly.

Nick looked at him and thought for a moment. "Of course you're invited," Nick said.

Cuthbert smiled.

Nick continued, "It's Thanksgiving, there is always room for another turkey."

Bob and Nick laughed...Cuthbert did not.

Chapter 21

Nick awoke early on Thanksgiving Day, as he always did. Mary, his daughter, liked to get up and have cinnamon rolls, waffles, and hot chocolate for breakfast, then her mom and dad would watch the Thanksgiving Day parades. Then they would watch *Miracle on 34th Street* before getting ready to go to her Grandpa Billy's for Thanksgiving. It was a good day, as all of her aunts, uncles, and cousins from both her mom and dad's families would be there and later her adopted uncles Bart and Jonathan would arrive, if the Bears were playing in Chicago.

Nick continued this ritual, but over the years it had just been Duke and Tina, then Duke, then Duke, Baron and Ruby. Sometimes, he didn't make it over to Billy's because the memories made it too hard. When He didn't attend, Bart and Jonathon always came by in the evening just because they were his friends.

This Thanksgiving, he would go to Billy's and bring the A...un...gel...s with him, screw it.

Nick was making the waffles with Baron and Ruby watching carefully to ensure that he got everything right.

Bob wandered into the kitchen and poured coffee and sat at the kitchen table.

"How is she?" Nick asked, his voice breaking a little.

"She is fine, they are both fine. She is worried about you," Bob said. "She feels responsible for the change in you," Bob said.

"What change would that be?" Nick asked.

"She was so proud when you cleared Tim McCarty's name," Bob said. "She was proud when you saved that Episcopal priest, and she was sad when Duke passed, but when she saw him again, well a girl and her dogs, and his sister Tina was overjoyed to see him. But she was the first to see the change in you. You didn't laugh anymore, at least not much. You still kidded around, but she saw the anger underneath it.

She saw you withdraw from her Grandpa and Uncle Wil. She saw you spiraling down in despair and losing hope and she felt it was because of her.

"I hope someone told her it wasn't her fault," Nick said.

"There was your mom and others," Bob said. "You frightened her when you got shot, and it didn't seem you tried to avoid it."

"I didn't mean to scare her," Nick said.

"She knew, we all knew," Bob said. "You let your grief and pain turn you away. You wake up every morning with sorrow and pain, which is followed by anger and revenge."

"Well, it's over now," Nick said.

Cuthbert walked in. "Is it, Nick? Is it over?"

"The men who were responsible are in jail or have been punished," Nick said.

"True, some are in jail and some you turned your back on and let Antonio take care of it," Cuthbert said.

"You didn't take care of it yourself, but you had an idea what Antonio might do," Cuthbert said. "This would be an excellent time for you to say, 'you aren't your brother's keeper,' Nick."

Nick looked at him.

"Yum, waffles, cinnamon rolls and hot chocolate," Cuthbert said.

Baron and Ruby sat on the couch waiting to see if Nick would share. Cuthbert and Bob sat in chairs and they all watched the parade. Then they watched *Miracle on 34th Street.*

"You know, I look a little like Edmund Gwenn," Cuthbert said.

"No, you don't," Bob said.

"I wish they had sent Edmund Gwenn," Nick said.

"Hey, I heard that," Cuthbert said.

"Good," Nick replied.

"Nick, I have to talk to you about something that I have been instructed to do," Cuthbert said.

"Do you really think this is the time?" Bob asked.

"No time like the present," Cuthbert said.

"Nick, I have found your older sister," Cuthbert said.

"Where is she," Nick asked.

"We can't tell you," Bob said.

"Why," Nick said.

"We feel it wouldn't..." Bob was interrupted.

"She doesn't want us to; she doesn't want to see any of you; she wants no part of this family now or ever," Cuthbert said.

"Cuthbert, you could have been a little kinder," Bob said.

"Nick didn't need to have it kinder; he tells it like it is, no niceties for Nick, he's a straight shooter, you know like he was with the Turley boys," Cuthbert said. "Bob, did you know that he scared those two to the point they considered trying to find a way to kill themselves. Didn't know that, did you? Tough guy, and to boot he got his younger brother to do it too."

"Enough, Cuthbert," Bob said.

"Oh, that's right, you're his guardian angel. See, Nick, I can say it. You protect old Nick here from those who may harm him. Bob, who protects everyone else from Nick these days," Cuthbert said. "How did you get from clearing McCarty, to finding Joe Lang's killer, to clearing Tracey Donavon and Kurt Murray's murders after forty years, to torturing people in a basement?"

"Why don't you get out and leave me alone?" Nick said.

"I would be happy to. Do you think I enjoyed the kid that threw up on me today because he was excited to see Santa? You think I like talking to you? I would be happy to go if you just answer my question, how did you get to where you are now? You answer that honestly and I'm out of here, but old Bob here is stuck with you."

The room went silent.

"Oh, look, Edmund Gwenn left his cane in the new house," Cuthbert said. "Got nothing, huh, Nick? When you do, let me know."

"Cuthbert, let it drop," Bob said, "now!"

"Not until I tell him what I have been instructed to do," Cuthbert said. "I have to ask your father and your brother Wil if they want to be reunited with your sister. They will probably say no, and it will hurt them, and I also have to encourage them to stop deceiving Phil and Laura."

"Why do you have to do that?" Nick asked. "That's just cruel."

"You should know, the past few years you have become an expert on cruel," Cuthbert said, "but I will answer your question, even if you won't answer mine. I will do it because you haven't. You, your father, and brother kept the secret so long that it is almost impossible to make it right. You have hurt your sister by never reaching out and you have hurt yourselves. Actions good or bad have consequences. I know and you know the reason behind your reaching out and including Katie, Greg and now Dom in your family is in part because you never tried to bring your sister back into the family."

Nick stood up and walked out of the room. Baron and Ruby followed.

Cuthbert looked at Bob and said, "That went well, don't you think?"

Bob looked him, "Yeah, I think, do you?"

"Tough love, baby, tough love," Cuthbert said. "Are there any more of those cinnamon rolls?"

Chapter 22

Nick, Bob, Baron, Ruby and Cuthbert piled into Nick's Edge to make the trip to Billy's. It was thirty-seven degrees outside of the car, but despite the heater turned up in the Edge, it was still much colder than the outside temperature. No one spoke a word until they arrived, and Billy opened the door to welcome them.

Billy opened the door wide and ushered everyone in. Baron and Ruby rushed through the door to be petted and made over by the rest of the family. Billy loved having his family and their friends come to his home.

Nick introduced Cuthbert and Bob to his father.

"Cuthbert Quigle?" Billy said.

"Yes." He looked into Billy's eyes and said, "It's a common name isn't it. We were friends of Nick at Michigan. I was his favorite professor."

"Yes, yes, it is a common name," Billy said. "You were friends of Nick at Michigan."

"Yes, I was in Nick's class and Cuthbert was one of our professors," Bob said.

Billy said, "You were one of Nick's favorite professors."

"I was," Cuthbert said, wide a wide smile.

Bob whispered to Cuthbert, "Will you stop doing that."

It was a large gathering. Nick didn't know that Sinclair Stewart had come up and so did Alex Papadakis and Casey Charlette, from the St. Louis office. Bob and Laura Wilson, Nick's sister and brother-in-law, also came up and brought the twins. Baron was sitting on the couch guarding them and the twins loved it.

"Hey Pop, Happy Thanksgiving," Katie said.

"Yeah," Nick said.

"I see you still have your house guests with you," she said.

"Yes, I do," Nick said.

"You know what Franklin said about house guests?" she asked.

"Yes," Nick said.

"Guests, like fish, begin to smell after three days," she said.

"Doesn't take that long," Nick replied. "Where's Greg?"

"Where's the food?" she laughed. "What's the story with those two?"

"They don't have a story; they are here to drive me out of my mind," Nick said.

"Short drive if you ask me," Nick's younger brother Phil said.

"What was that, Old Yeller?" Wil, his older brother asked.

"Not funny," Phil said. "I have to get back to my date."

"You do that. The grownups need to talk," Wil said.

"Grownups? That's a laugh," Phil said.

"Next month you want to be called Pinkie?" Wil asked.

Wil turned to Nick. "So who are these guys?"

"You heard, a friend from grad school and my former professor," Nick said.

"What kind of trouble are they in?" Wil asked.

"They're not in trouble. They are visiting," Nick responded.

"Okay, what kind of trouble are you in?"

"Well, if you must know, they have come down from heaven to save me from everlasting suffering in hell because of my trespasses against God, humanity and myself," Nick said.

"I'm serious, Nick," Wil said, with his best Jack Webb/Joe Friday detective voice.

"So, you want 'just the facts?'" Nick mocked.

"Do you want me to run a check on them?" Wil asked.

"Sure, make you sure you let me know what data base you're going to use," Nick said, with a laugh.

"What does that mean?" Wil asked.

"Wil, Bob was a friend in grad school and Cuthbert was the most eccentric professor at the university. I knew them a while ago. This is no big deal," Nick said.

"There is something not right about those two," Wil said.

"Tell me about it," Nick said.

"What are they really doing here?" Wil pressed.

"They are taking a holiday trip. Bob is taking in the sites and Cuthbert got himself a job for the holidays as a mall Santa," Nick said.

"What, a mall Santa, why?' Wil asked.

"Sociologist," Nick said.

"Oh," Wil said, and that seemed to satisfy him.

Nick was surprised, until he turned around and saw Cuthbert standing behind Wil smiling that irritating cat-that-swallowed-the-canary smile. "Will you stop doing that?"

"I have to protect the mission," Cuthbert replied with a movie-style spy demeanor.

"Was that a line from a cloak and dagger film?" Nick asked.

"It's probably been used before in a book or movie," Cuthbert said. "You know, Nick, you are not nearly as big of an ass as I thought you would be."

"Well, thank you, Cuthbert. You are exactly as big of an ass as I thought you would be," Nick said.

"Touchy," Cuthbert said.

"Don't you mean touché," Nick asked.

"No," Cuthbert said. "I meant you're a touchy twit who has crawled into a hole where your kind don't enjoy anything in your life, not this wonderful family, not these interesting people you call friends, not your success. I know you weren't always a nitwit like this."

"Thanks," Nick said.

"I didn't say you weren't always a nitwit. I said you were not always a nitwit...like this," Cuthbert said, smiling.

"Thank you for the clarification," Nick said.

"You're welcome. Buck up, my boy, I could have said that you were a dope or a numbskull or a dolt or a dunce or blockhead," Cuthbert said.

"Well, thank you for that," Nick responded.

"All of which is accurate to describe how you have been living your life...I could have also called you a prick, based on some of your exploits."

"Well, Happy Thanksgiving to you too," Nick said.

Cuthbert smiled. "Right back at ya, Prick..., I mean Nick."

Nick was about to reply when Bob walked up. "Having a good time?" he asked.

Nick looked at him and walked away.

"Cuthbert, what happened."

"Tough love, Bob, tough love." Cuthbert smiled.

"Why don't you and I mingle a little, several others have arrived, and we should get to know the people he cares about and the people who care about him," Bob said. "Oh, has he asked any of the questions yet?"

"No, but he will, and my guess is he will before Christmas," Cuthbert said. "This is going to be more difficult than I thought."

"Not more difficult than I thought," Bob said. "I've been with him from the beginning and through everything with him. He was a good kid but never got a lot of encouragement from Billy. He was just second to Wil, and that made him independent. He was an idealistic kid. I was with him when he lost his children, and his heart was broken. And I was with him when Annie, his wife and grade school sweetheart, left, which broke what was left of his heart. That's when I began to believe there would be trouble down the line."

"Down the line?" Cuthbert asked.

"I could see he was beginning to change. In some ways it was good because he took cases that meant something, but at the same time there was a darkness growing. It's not uncommon with those who are bombarded with the worst

91

humanity has to give every day. Some become jaded, some become vengeful, some just give up, some bury it deep until it destroys them inside, and some find their spirit and come to understand that the important thing is to have hope."

"Which do think our boy is?" Cuthbert asked.

Bob smiled sadly. "I don't know, I believe he still has some hope left in him, but I don't know. We are going to have to access the people in his life and we are going to have to do that not through Nick's eyes but through their eyes. Nick has misplaced the ability to feel much but anger, pain, and loss."

"I told him he was a prick," Cuthbert said, almost sadly.

"Not the best way to wish someone a Happy Thanksgiving," Bob said. "You going to tell him about the cop?"

"I don't know," Cuthbert said.

"That's why you took on this assignment, wasn't it," Bob said. "You should at some point, as it could make a difference. Let's go mingle."

Chapter 23

Billy's home was a large brick house on the northside that was built by his late wife's grandfather, one of the few members of Nick's family that was not in law enforcement. It is the house that his wife grew up in and the house that his children grew up in.

Billy's dining room and sunroom was set up like a homey cabaret. There was a buffet table with food at one end of the dining room. The dining room table was in the middle of the room surrounded by smaller tables that extended into the sunroom and spilled over into part of the living room. The island in the kitchen was set up as a bar with tall chairs around it; that of course was where Nick, Sinclair and Wil were sitting.

Right before the call for dinner was given, Bart and Jonathon arrived from "da Bears" game. A few minutes later Felix Coughlin and Constance Trebble arrived with Mrs. Marbulls. Hail, hail the gangs all here. Laura, Katie, and Casey were apparently in charge of the feast, but once Mrs. Marbulls arrived, she took command to ensure that things would run smoothly.

Finally, Billy tapped his glass and asked everyone to find a seat. Everyone did. Mrs. Marbulls made sure that Nick, Sinclair, and Wil moved from the kitchen to the dining room.

Billy gave his Thanksgiving speech, "Friends, I am very happy that you have chosen to spend this evening with our family, because you are not only good friends, but you are also part of this family, so welcome. Since last Thanksgiving we have all faced some very difficult challenges and we have all have come through the obstacles that we faced, as grave as they may have been, stronger. We should be thankful that we are here this evening together, sharing a meal and sharing each other's company and fellowship.

I have asked one of our new friends to give the blessing, Cuthbert."

"Thank you, Mr. Caldwell," Cuthbert said.

Bob looked at Nick. Nick picked up his glass and downed it.

"Bob and I are friends of Nick's from the university. We are on a pilgrimage, this holiday season, and it is an adventure that we hope can bring hope and peace to those we meet in our travels. If you would all bow your heads. "Dear Father, we ask that you bless this gathering of good people; that you bless the food that you have provided." He looked at the twins. "Bless these children and we know that you will bless these splendid pups that show love to all with no reservation. Bless the Caldwell family, all the Caldwell family, those with us this evening and those who are not. As we move into the Christmas season let us remember not only the symbols of Christmas but also the reason for that celebration, the coming of your Son. May you grant us peace and may we feel your love for us through this season and throughout the coming year. Amen. Let's eat."

"Wonderful," Billy said.

There were smiles all around.

Nick picked up Sinclair's drink and downed it.

After the meal was done and dessert was served, people gathered in groups and told stories about past Thanksgivings and Christmases. Baron and Ruby curled up on the couch with Nick and Sinclair.

"Who are those guys?" Sinclair asked.

"House guests," Nick replied.

"No, I'm serious, who are they?" Sinclair pressed.

"They're guys I knew in Ann Arbor," Nick said.

"They're not writing a book about you, are they?" Sinclair asked.

"No," Nick said, "Why?"

Sinclair said, "Well, it seems like every conversation they are having is about you."

"It's nothing," Nick said.

"It's creepy," Sinclair said.

"I know, they're sociologists/psychologists," Nick said. "They like to listen to stories about people."

"I think they're damn nosey," Sinclair said.

"Yeah, I told you they're sociologists/psychologists," Nick said, "so that would make them nosey and rude."

"If they were any weirder or irritating, they would be lawyers." Sinclair said.

"No, that would be me, I'm a lawyer," Nick said, with a laugh.

Sinclair said, "No, you are a detective with a law degree. You're weird and irritating because you are you."

"Screw off, old man," Nick said, and they both laughed. "They think I should start practicing law."

"What the hell for?" Sinclair asked.

"Because I am already weird and irritating, so I might as well since I have two of the essential tools." They laughed again.

"No, really, why do they think you should practice law?" Sinclair asked.

"So I could do good," Nick said.

"So you could do good?" Sinclair asked.

"Yeah, can we just stop talking about this? It is interrupting my drinking," Nick said.

"Do you know what I think?" Sinclair said.

"I never have," Nick said.

"I'm serious," Sinclair said. "I think you need to do a background check on those two."

"You do, huh, that's a good idea," Nick said. "Why don't you do it? I would be interested in what you find."

"Oh, I almost forgot," Sinclair said, "before I left New Orleans, I was doing some of my Christmas shopping on that Amazon thingy, when I saw something that I thought you would like. I want to get you something else for Christmas, but I thought I would get this just because I knew it is something that you would really like."

"That Amazon thingy?" Nick said.

"Yeah, you know, the place you go on the computer and buy stuff you don't need," Sinclair said.

"I know what Amazon is," Nick said.

"Well, I got you this," Sinclair said as he pulled out an Amazon mailing packet.

He handed the pouch to Nick. Nick looked at him and said, "You shouldn't have."

"I couldn't resist," he said.

Nick opened it and it was two books, the titles were, *"When Christmas Trees Flew"* and a detective story, *"Dead Crowe."* Nick looked at Sinclair. "Really?"

"I knew you would love them," Sinclair laughed, "since they are both by your favorite author. Oh, on the way up, I stopped in St. Louis and got them signed for you." Sinclair laughed again. "The Christmas one isn't bad, but I knew you would really like the detective story. It's about this brooding self-involved but brilliant detective who is generally a pain in the ass to everyone who comes in contact with him."

"I think I have read a couple of the other books this guy wrote," Nick said.

"You have?" Sinclair said with a smile.

"Yeah, he usually works his cases with this senile old bastard from New Orleans," Nick said.

Sinclair laughed. "Don't you mean he works his cases with a terribly handsome senile old bastard from New Orleans?"

"No," Nick said.

Chapter 24

Over the next two weeks communication between Nick and Cuthbert was more like sparring with Bob as referee. This was accompanied by heavy drinking. Nick did his best to make sure he wasn't the topic of conversation.

"So," Nick said, "if Adam and Eve were the first two people and their sons were people three and four, where did their wives come from?"

"Are you kidding me?" Cuthbert asked. "What? Do you have the intellect and curiosity of an eight-year-old in Sunday school?"

"You're should know this stuff, you're an A...un...gel...s, screw it," Nick said. "Why can't I say that here when no one is here but us?" A...un...gel...s

Cuthbert smiled, "Rules is rules, chump." Then he laughed. "What else you got?"

Nick, being a jerk, asked, "How many A...un...gel...s can dance on the head of a pin?"

"How many of what," Cuthbert said, "can dance on the head of a pin? I don't know how many A...un...gel...s can dance on the head of a pin and if you meant Angels...no one really gives a damn how many can unless Joe Biden does."

"Okay, what about the wedding?" Nick asked.

"What wedding?" Cuthbert replied.

"You know, the wedding where one of your bosses turned water into wine. How did he do that?" Nick said.

"Who do you think he is, Penn or Teller? My Lord, and you are the product of a Jesuit education. I'm surprised some Jesuit didn't beat the crap out of you," Cuthbert said.

"They kinda did," Nick said.

"Well, they shouldn't have hit you in the head so much," Cuthbert said.

"You haven't answered my question," Nick insisted.

"Okay, but you can't tell anybody. He had this wineskin under his cloak and when no one was looking he emptied the entire wineskin into the jugs," Cuthbert said.

"Really," Nick said.

"No, you dumb ass, he is the Son of God, it was a miracle. Are you as dumb as you seem, or are you drunk, or both?" Cuthbert asked.

"Hey, inquiring minds want to know," Nick slurred.

"Bob, have you been listening to this idiot?" Cuthbert asked.

"What? Oh, no, I'm watching this movie, *Desperado*, admiring the work of the Boss," Bob replied.

"What?" Cuthbert asked.

"The Boss knew what he was doing when he created her," Bob said.

"What are you talking about?" Cuthbert asked.

"This actress, Salma Hayek, and she likes milk too," Bob said cheerfully. "Nick, may I ask you a question?"

"Shoot," Nick said.

"I thought you'd be tired of getting shot, Nick," Bob said.

"No, I meant what's your question?" Nick said.

"She wouldn't happen to live in Chicago, would she?" Bob asked.

"No, she lives in Hollywood probably," Nick said.

"Hollywood, not even Lucifer would go there," Bob said.

"Funny, I would have thought he would feel at home out there. Anyway, speaking of Satan," Nick said, "How come your Boss and that Arch A...un...gel, guy Michael couldn't finish him off?"

"Nick, we don't talk about Satan and we don't criticize the Boss, as you put it, or Michael," Bob said.

"Why?" Nick asked.

Bob said, "Well, because..." he was interrupted by Cuthbert.

"We don't criticize Michael because he has little sense of humor and he might come down here and reach down your throat and pull you inside out, and that would be only if he was in a good mood," Cuthbert said.

A voice from the couch said, "That's true, he is a fierce warrior, and he protects those who fight evil; he has probably protected you. Every Halloween the last hour of the day and the first hour of All Saints he protects the BearhounDs that fight evil on the cosmic plane to protect peoplekind. It's Michael's spirit that protects us," Baron said.

Cuthbert looked at Baron. "Very true and thank you."

"It's our job," Baron said.

"No problem, we like to kick evil's butt," Ruby exclaimed, "It's fun."

"I think I need another drink," Nick said.

"I think you need to get your head out of your butt and make an effort to understand that we are all here to help you," Cuthbert said. "Nick, what do you want? I mean what do you really want? What will it take for you to pull down that wall you hide behind and realize you are loved and valued and have a lot of good work to do before your time is done here?"

Nick looked at him. He looked as if he had a tear in his eye and started to speak, "You don't have the steam or the push." Nick got up and left the room.

Cuthbert looked at Bob, "This is looking like it is hopeless."

"He's right, we don't have the power to give him what he wants," Bob said.

"What does he want?" Cuthbert said. "The Boss sent us here to bring him back into the fold?"

"He wants Mary and little Wil back," Baron said. "Can you do that?"

"No, we can't, Baron," Bob said. "I'm sorry."

"Come on, Ruby, bedtime," Baron said.

The two pups walked out of the room, both with their heads bowed, looking very sad, and headed off to be with Nick.

Cuthbert and Bob sat and looked at the fire. They didn't speak, but the little pups' words had touched them both.

"We can't do that, right," Cuthbert asked.

A sad smile crossed Bob's face. "No, Cuth, we can't do that, and Nick knows we can't do that."

"If he knows that, maybe that's not what he really wants," Cuthbert said. "Maybe that is his wish, but Nick is a pragmatic guy. May be he really wants something else."

"Like what?" Bob asked.

"Well, if we can't bring them back, then maybe he wants to go there to see them," Cuthbert said.

"He will see them again one day, when his time here is done," Bob said

"What if he has been trying to hurry that along? I mean the guy gets shot a lot," Cuthbert replied.

"He knows better. If he tries anything like that, I mean deliberately putting himself in harm's way to get to eternity early, why the intent is the same as suicide," Bob said. "If he does that, he will never see them again. Besides, he knows better, he knows the rules."

"Is there anything we can do?" Cuthbert said.

"I can't think of anything," Bob said. "Let me make a call, I have an idea."

Chapter 25

The next morning Nick got up early and fed Baron and Ruby. Then he proceeded to fix breakfast for his guests. He was touched by the concern that both Cuthbert and Bob had shown the night before. He was tired and he suspected that he was tired because of the anger he had held since the day he lost his family. After all, it was his fault because of the job he had and that he wasn't there to stop it. He had carried this pain, this guilt, this shame for a long time. He trusted it. He believed in some strange way it was what made him effective. He also knew it was destroying him.

Bob came into the kitchen and sat at the table.

"Want some coffee?" Nick asked.

"Sure," Bob said. "Did you get any sleep?"

"A few hours," Nick said. "Where's our friend?"

"He'll be along," Bob replied.

"You know, Nick, Cuthbert was chosen to come here because he suffered in the same way you have when he was alive," Bob said.

Nick didn't respond.

"He lost his family, but unlike you he was to blame. He had a good heart like you, but he wouldn't have been considered a good man," Bob said, "You're a good man with a broken heart. He took this assignment because of another good man who tried to help him, and you remind him of that man."

"Who do I remind him of?" Nick said.

"He was a Chicago policeman too. Cuthbert failed at almost everything he did. As you have probably figured out, he battles the one thing that almost kept him out of heaven," Bob said.

"What would that be?" Nick asked.

"His pride," Bob replied, "but as I said, he had a good heart but no ability to right himself. This officer tried to help, but Cuthbert was ashamed that he couldn't provide and take

101

care of his family, so he turned to self-destructive behavior. He left his family and began to drink himself to death. This officer tried to get him to stop and go back to his family, but the shame and embarrassment of what he had become overpowered him, and he lost hope. This officer found him in an alley drunk, sick, and dying. He called a priest and held him while the priest gave him the last rites of his faith. Before he died, he asked for forgiveness and he received it. He asked the officer to look after his family and to tell them he was sorry and that he loved them. He died in the officer's arms before they could get him to a hospital. It was Christmas Eve."

"Did the officer contact his family?" Nick asked.

"The officer did. Cuthbert's wife and little daughter were devastated; they loved him even with his flaws. His daughter prayed for him to go to heaven, and children's prayers carry a lot of weight with the Boss, as you call him. Cuthbert got into heaven because that little girl prayed for her daddy and his wife prayed for him and the officer prayed for him until the day he died."

"What happened to his family?" asked.

"They survived largely because the officer kept his word. He looked out for them. He found a job for the wife and he became like an uncle to the girl, much like you have for Katie and Greg. He even gave Cuthbert's daughter away at her wedding, and he was the godfather of her first child. Before the officer passed on, he asked his son who was also a Chicago police officer to continue to watch over Cuthbert's family, and that officer asked his son to continue to check on them."

Nick asked, "Why did Cuthbert feel he was a failure, what did he do?"

"Cuthbert was a painter and not a bad one at that. He did street scenes of Chicago, but he sold very few paintings and destroyed most of them when he was drunk. In fact, only a couple of them have survived. One of them I believe hangs in his great granddaughter's home, and his widow gave the other one to the officer who tried to save him."

"Do you know the officer's name?" Nick asked.

Cuthbert walked into the kitchen. "What are you two doing, swapping recipes?"

"No," Bob said, "we were discussing how the White Sox would do this year since they hired Tony La Russa as manager."

"I have heard about him from a guy who was playing a harmonica at the coffee shop, Stan something," Cuthbert said.

"Musial?" Nick asked.

"Something like that. He said this Tony guy really loved dogs," Cuthbert said. "What's for breakfast? I have a long day at the mall."

"Where are our gifts?" Nick asked.

"Gifts?" Cuthbert responded, "it's not Christmas and you have been naughty, so no gifts."

"It's December 6th, St. Nicholas Day, and St. Nicholas is supposed to bring little gifts and candy and put them in our shoes," Nick said.

"That's the dumbest thing I have ever heard of," Cuthbert said.

Cuthbert's cell phone rang. He answered it.

They heard a loud voice on the other end of the call.

"Yes sir...I know sir...yes sir, I do know brand is important...yes sir...no sir...yes sir...no sir I do not want to end up in the stable...I will sir," Cuthbert said. "No sir, it won't happen again...and Ho, Ho, Ho, to you too, sir."

Cuthbert walked to the kitchen table and picked up a plate and turned to Nick and handed it to him. "Happy St. Nicholas day, here's your gift."

"You are giving my plate to me as a gift?" Nick asked.

"How observant you are; no wonder you're a world class detective," Cuthbert said. "Since you have that gift plate in your hand could you fill it with some eggs and four strips of bacon, please?"

"We like bacon," Baron said.

"Yeah, we like bacon a lot," Ruby said.

103

Cuthbert looked at Nick. "Could you make that eight strips of bacon and two chew sticks?"

Chapter 26

Mrs. Marbulls began reciting the calls that Nick would have to return that morning as soon as he walked in. Baron and Ruby circled Mrs. Marbulls' desk and sat. They were waiting for their morning treat. Upon receiving it they sauntered into Nick's office and took their positions on the coach.

Nick sat at his desk and Mrs. Marbulls' voice came over the intercom, instructing him to "Return those calls...NOW."

The first call was to his brother, Wil.

"What's up," Nick asked.

"I've been checking into your two house guests," Wil announced.

Nick smiled. "What did you find out?"

"Nothing on your friend Bob," Wil said. It's like he never existed. But for your former professor, I found a lot."

"Really?" Nick said.

"I found out a lot. The guy was detained for public drunkenness, vagrancy, and illegal peddling. There is more. Apparently, this 'Cuthbert Quigle was a painter," Wil said.

Nick asked, "Houses? Fences? The town?"

"Nick, not everything is funny," Wil said. "I worry about you sometimes."

"Me too," Nick said.

"This guy painted landscapes of the city but never got traction. He left his family and wandered the city," Wil said.

"Is there any information about his family?" Nick asked.

"You know I don't like it when you ask me to violate department regulations," Wil said. "So what time are you coming over?"

"This afternoon," Nick said.

"Wait, Nick, there is something weird here. Cuthbert Quigle died at the age of thirty-two," Wi said.

Nick smiled, "Well, we know this isn't the same guy. I just left him a while ago and he was eating eggs and getting ready to go play Santa at the mall."

In an ominous tone, Wil said, "Nick, he died on Christmas Eve in 1927."

"Wow, he really looks good for his age; he would be about, what a hundred - twenty-five years old," Nick said. "I'm going to have pay more attention to what he eats."

"There is something fishy, here," Wil added.

Nick said, "You think? I agree, but you have to admit he looks good and gets around pretty good for a guy who died, what something like ninety-three years ago...Thanks, Wil. I'll see you later."

The next call was to the great New Orleans P. I., Sinclair Stewart, who could be contacted at NOLADick.com, or something like that. Sinclair and Bart were Nick's closest and most trusted friends.

"You called?" Nick asked.

"Yeah that character at your house is..."

"A painter? Died ninety-three years ago? And is one hundred-twenty-five years old? Left his family? Was a drunk, a vagrant and a peddler of art that no one bought?" Nick asked.

"Okay, smart ass, you talked to your brother already," Sinclair said. "I'm going to look into this a little more. Wil is sending me a copy of this Cuthbert Quigle's file."

"He's sending a copy of the file to you?" Nick asked. "He's breaking Chicago P.D. regulations and sending you a copy of the file, and he is making me come over and look at the file at his office. I don't believe him."

"Well, I think I can help you with some insight on this. First of all, I have the time to thoroughly look through the file, he doesn't. Second, I'm cool and dashing and you are a pain in the ass," Sinclair said. "I'll call you after I look at the file."

"You really are a NOLA Dick, aren't you," Nick said.

"You bet your ass," Sinclair said. "Hey, you be careful around those two. There is definitely something wrong with them."

The call ended and Nick gave a little laugh. "You don't know the half of it."

Chapter 27

Bob went to the Mall to see Cuthbert. He waited until the afternoon break.

"Ho, Ho, Ho, Santa's got to take a little break to feed the reindeer," Cuthbert said.

One of his helper "elves" said, "Don't worry kids, Santa will be back in thirty minutes."

"We have to talk," Bob said.

"Do you know what the worst part of being in human form is?" Cuthbert asked.

"Having to go to the bathroom?" Bob replied.

Cuthbert stopped and looked at him and said, "Yeah, I'll be right back." And there went Santa sprinting through the mall to get to the men's room.

Bob was waiting for him when he walked out. "Did you come up with anything?"

"No, I thought you were supposed be the brains of the outfit," Cuthbert said.

"I am," Bob said. "But I came up with nothing. This is clearly out of our pay grade."

"We get paid?" Cuthbert asked with a smile.

"You know what I mean," Bob said.

Cuthbert asked, "So, what are we going to do?"

"We're going to call for some assistance," Bob said.

"To whom?" Cuthbert asked nervously.

"I'm going to ask for guidance from Uriel," Bob said.

"Are you crazy? He won't have time to come here and help," Cuthbert said.

"He is very gracious with his time. Think of him as a celestial consultant. We asked him to provide us with some options; besides, I copied "J" on the message. Remember Mary and little Wil asked "J" to help their daddy. I am sure that he will encourage Urial to help," Bob said. "Urial is the ultimate voice when it comes to decision making. He is known as the angel of wisdom. He shines the light of the Boss's truth into the darkness of confusion.

"The faithful turn to Uriel for help seeking the Boss's will before making decisions, learning new information, solving problems, and resolving conflicts. We turn to him for help letting go of destructive emotions such as anxiety and anger, which can prevent us from discerning wisdom or recognizing dangerous situations."

Cuthbert looked at Bob. "You've been looking stuff up on Nick's computer, haven't you?"

"Well," Bob said.

"You've been on that Internet thing again, haven't you?" Cuthbert said. "Have you ever heard of the First Commandment?"

Bob said, "But the article said it so much better than I could. I was rehearsing in case I had to explain it to Nick."

"When is he coming?" Cuthbert asked.

"Nick's working on some investigation and won't get back until late. I thought I would get him here this evening," Bob said.

"Do we have to cook, because neither of us do that well?" Cuthbert said.

"He's an arch angel," Bob said.

"Well, I'll order some pizza and pick up some soda on the way home, to be on the safe side. What are you going to do?" Cuthbert asked.

"I thought I would spend the afternoon meditating," Bob said.

"Really, where would you do this meditating?" Cuthbert asked.

"I thought I might do it at The Art Institute," Bob said.

"The Art Institute?" Cuthbert asked.

"Okay, the Clark Street Ale House," Bob said.

"And people consider me a lush," Cuthbert said.

"Hey, angels can't get drunk," Bob said.

Cuthbert said, "Tell me about it. I gotta get back to Toy Land."

Chapter 28

Nick sat in his office going over Cuthbert's file, which his brother sent over despite telling him he couldn't and wouldn't get a copy of the file and he would have to read it at Chicago P.D. Wil sent one over because that's what a big brother does for his little brother when he has an opportunity.

Ruby and Baron were enjoying the last few pieces of pizza crust from the pizza Nick ordered so he didn't have go out.

There was nothing that unusual about the file. Several times Cuthbert had been detained for public drunkenness, but he had only been arrested and charged twice. All the times that he had been detained it was a young officer named Andrew Caldwell that brought him in. On the two occasions he was arrested for public drunkenness the officer involved was not Andrew Caldwell.

Cuthbert was also arrested for arson, but Officer Caldwell got the charge reduced. Cuthbert had set fire to a number of his paintings behind his house. He of course was drunk, and Andrew was able to find a friendly judge whose name was MacGill. Judge Cameron MacGill was tough on big crimes but empathetic toward those down on their luck. Judge MacGill always found a way to lighten the load on Cuthbert. Of course, Judge MacGill was also very proud of his nephew, Andy Caldwell...the Chicago way.

He also found out that Cuthbert was a regular guest at several precinct holdovers around the city. Thanks to Judge MacGill's empathy word spread that Cuthbert was not to sleep in alleys. Someone always would ask why this drunk, angry, sad man was given obvious preferential treatment.

Well, Bob was wrong. There were a few more of Cuthbert's paintings that survived the bonfire behind his garage, and if anyone took the time when visiting Judge MacGill to look closely at a painting they would have seen the initials "CQ" in the lower right-hand corner of a painting of

Comiskey Park that hung behind the Judge's desk in Chambers. Judge MacGill was a fan. That painting today hangs in the office of his uncles and cousins' law offices at MacGill and Caldwell. A firm that Billy, Nick's father, believes is where all the black sheep of the family dwell, and if being lawyers weren't bad enough, they were criminal defense attorneys. Billy also blames two of his brothers for Nick quitting the force and going to law school. Billy and his brothers stopped speaking when his brothers Wallace and Alexander offered Nick a place at the firm when he graduated from Michigan. Nick turned it down to pursue a career as a private investigator, another career that his father believed was as bad as being a criminal defense attorney.

Nick thought about all this and realized for some reason this crazy "ang," never mind, Cuthbert, was a small part of his family history.

Nick read everything in the file. He called an old friend who was a professor of history--Chicago history to be more specific--at Loyola, Dr. Michael Butler.

"Mike, sorry to call you at home," Nick said.

"Nick?" Butler asked. "Well, how have you been? I've been thinking about you since I read that you solved your daughter's case, congratulations."

"Thanks, Mike," Nick said.

"What can I do for you," Butler said.

"I am working on a cold case and I need to trace someone's family and find any living relatives that might still be around," Nick said.

"What's the name?" Butler asked.

"Cuthbert Quigle," Nick said.

Nick was shocked when Butler asked, "The artist?"

"Yeah, you heard of him?" Nick asked.

"Well, I know the name, he did landscapes of the city. He wasn't bad, but not much of his work survived, if any," Butler said. "He died pretty young."

"Christmas Eve, 1927," Nick said.

"Can you give me a few days; I'll see what I can find out and call you back." Butler said.

"Thanks, Mike," Nick said.

"Hey, I rarely get to do something like this; it will be fun. Good night, Nick; I'll start on this in the morning," Butler said.

Baron and Ruby were not in any hurry to head home. They were snuggled in blankets on opposite ends of the couch. They had dinner and a special treat of pizza crust, and they were taken care of by someone who loved them. Their lives were good. If only that were true for all of us.

Chapter 29

Cuthbert burst through the door, with arms full of pizza, chips, dip, and Coke Zero and headed for the kitchen.

"Bob, I'm going to put the pizza in the oven to keep it warm. What time do you think he will be here?"

"Cuthbert," Bob said.

"I hope he likes onion dip and chips," Cuthbert said.

"I don't know, I don't think I have ever had onion dip," an unfamiliar voice said.

Cuthbert turned and saw a very tall, muscular man, with a square jaw, blonde hair, and the clearest blue eyes that Cuthbert had ever seen. He looked at Bob who looked like he was standing at attention.

"Hi, I'm Cuthbert."

"I gathered that. I understand why you were chosen for this assignment," Uriel said.

"Really," Cuthbert said.

"Yes," Uriel said, "You have a very strong resemblance to St. Nicholas."

"You know, I was watching an old movie, *The Three Musketeers,* on TV, and if they ever decided to make a movie about you, they should cast a young Richard Chamberlain to play you," Cuthbert said.

"Go on, Cuthbert," Uriel said. "I know you want to say it; it's okay."

"Really?" Cuthbert said.

"Really," Uriel replied.

Cuthbert smiled and said, "Movie reference, how did you know...."

Uriel smiled.

"Oh," Cuthbert said and smiled. He turned to Bob and said, "Cool guy, huh?"

Bob looked toward heaven.

"I understand that you may need some guidance and advice on how to complete your assignment," Uriel said.

"That's correct," Bob said.

"What exactly are you troubled about? Nick seems like he is coming along fine," Uriel said.

"Fine?" Cuthbert blurted out. "He is the most stubborn person I have ever come in contact with, he is a wise a...," Cuthbert paused, "well, you know what I mean."

"Well then, you are the perfect one to bring him around, you understand him," Uriel said. "Have confidence and it is clear that you truly care about him," Uriel said, "and we know why."

"I do?" Cuthbert asked.

Uriel smiled kindly, "Of course you do. You want to repay the kindness Andrew showed you."

Cuthbert said, "I do?"

"My advice is to listen, and let him know that you care," Uriel said. "You are doing well, I know that. Nick has opened up, even though he may not show it. His anger is lessening. He is close to taking a step forward; you two have done that."

"But how do we get him to the finish line? Baron said he wants his children back," Cuthbert said.

"Baron is a wise pup, but we know that is not possible," Uriel said, "but I have an idea. Why don't you go and get the pizza out of the oven and we'll sit and talk this through."

Cuthbert got up to get the pizza. "Coke Zero?"

"Why not," Uriel said. "Oh, are there anchovies on the pizza?"

"Uh, no, it's pepperoni, onions and jalapenos," Cuthbert said.

"Perfect," Uriel said. "And, Cuthbert, relax, quit using your head and start using your heart."

"Thanks," Cuthbert said.

"Oh, Cuthbert," Uriel said, "why don't you bring the onion dip and chips out too."

Chapter 30

It took Mike Butler two days to get back to Nick.

"Nick, I have good news for you," Mike said.

"That's refreshing for a change. Usually we don't get a lot of good news around here," Nick said.

"Well, when your job is primarily dealing with bad people and crime, old or current, I wouldn't think the news would be that good even if you solved a case," Mike said, "but this is different. We have a chance to enlighten a family on their family history. What a wonderful Christmas gift; you'll be giving a family good news."

"That's great, but what are you talking about specifically," Nick asked.

"Oh, I forgot that you're like those television detectives, you know, 'Just the facts ma'am.' I love those shows. You know, even though you were a police officer when you were in my classes, I never thought you would ever choose to be a private eye," Mike said.

"Mike, what did you find out?" Nick said.

"Well, over the last couple days, I think I have been able to accurately chart our late great and tragic artist's family tree. I also have some surprising news about your family, too," Mike said.

"My grandfather, Andrew, knew Cuthbert Quigle," Nick said.

"You are a good detective," Mike said.

"Thanks, but I had help from a guy I went to grad school with," Nick said.

"But Nick, they weren't friends; for some reason, your grandfather kept getting Cuthbert out of trouble. He was with him when he died in the street. It looks like he arranged and paid for the funeral," Mike said. "Do you know what the connection was between them?"

"Not a clue," Nick said.

"Well, he took care of him like a brother and after your Cuthbert died, he took care of Cuthbert's family. After Andrew's death, your dad took over until he left the force," Mike said, "and now…"

"Wil watches over them," Nick said.

"That's right," Mike said.

"He never mentioned it," Nick said. "How did you find all this out?

"Records, my boy, records. Follow the paper trail, as you coppers say." Mike laughed.

"Former copper, what paper trail?" Nick asked.

"Years ago," Mike said, "Andrew, with a few other police, started a fund for families in Chicago who lost what he called a key family member. Cuthbert's family was the first. They helped with schooling, medical expenses and miscellaneous items."

"What kind of miscellaneous items?" Nick asked.

"Oh, first communion clothes, birthday presents, school supplies, things like that. Oh, Christmas presents and a lunch for the little kids with Santa at the Old Chicago Club," Mike said.

"How did they fund it?" Nick asked.

"Well, that's interesting; it was typical Chicago." Mike laughed.

"It was funded by two groups. Many were and are members of the Chicago Police Department, and the other group was often the focus of the Chicago Police Department." Mike laughed again. "Only in Chicago."

"What do you mean?" Nick asked.

"Well, Nick, way back in the day your grandfather had a close schoolboy friend who took a much different path than your grandad, which was disappointing to your grandfather, particularly when he had to arrest him. I am sure your father had the same disappointment, as he had to arrest his father's boyhood friend's son." Mike laughter even louder.

"No, not…" Nick said.

116

"Bingo, the Carrandini family and several other of the families who pitched in to support the fund." Mike laughed again. "The Chicago Police and the old crime families were not partners-in-crime but were partners in Key Fund--that's what they called it and still do. This all predates the United Way."

"Mike, I never knew about this, not from dad and not from Joey, and I solved his uncle's murder," Nick said.

"Not surprising. They don't talk about this. Can you imagine what the vultures in the press would do with this? I can see the headline: COPS AND GANGSTERS IN BED WITH WIDOWS AND ORPHANS." Mike laughed again. "How could they explain it in a way that didn't look like they were in cahoots with each other?"

"Some them were in cahoots with each other," Nick said.

"True," Mike said, "but that proves my point, doesn't it?"

"What else did you find out?" Nick asked.

"I have the Quigle family tree from Cuthbert to his great, great granddaughter, Emily. Interested?" Mike asked.

"Emily?" Nick asked.

"Yep," Mike said. "She's four and in preschool. I have a picture I am sending you."

"I'm getting worried, where did you get a picture of a four-year-old girl?" Nick asked.

"She goes to the same preschool my son's kids go through...they send Christmas cards to the parents and grandparents," Mike said. "My daughter-in-law says that even at four, little Emily is an art savant. How do you like them apples?"

"Thanks, Mike, can you send over the picture and the family tree?" Nick asked.

"You'll have it this afternoon," he said. "You know, Nick, there's something magical about this."

"Maybe you're right, Mike," Nick said.

.

117

Chapter 31

Cuthbert was waiting for Nick when he arrived home after a long day. Baron and Ruby walked past Cuthbert and up the stairs to go to bed.

"Do you have a few minutes?" Cuthbert asked.

"For you, Cuthbert? No," Nick said, walking towards the stairs.

"Please, I need to speak with you," Cuthbert said.

Nick turned and sat in a chair. "What now?"

"Do you remember what the road to hell is paved with?" Cuthbert asked.

"Is this a trick question or just a dumb one?" Nick asked.

"Neither," Cuthbert said.

"Good intentions," Nick said.

"Correct. I'm afraid that my good intentions in trying to reach you have paved the way for failure in our mission," Cuthbert said.

"I would say that you made some good points at times," Nick said.

"Maybe," Cuthbert said, "but I think I made some serious mistakes."

"Like what?" Nick asked.

"I didn't listen," Cuthbert said. "Maybe if I had tried to understand."

"You know, I'm not the warmest person on earth," Nick said. "One of the things I have learned the hard way in my business was to really listen, and I lack compassion sometimes. When I was a cop, I didn't do that well at all. What I learned was that if I wanted to get information, I needed to listen, to empathize with the people I was interviewing and even those I was interrogating. I did a decent job of that until..."

"Until you lost your family," Cuthbert said.

Nick looked at him ready to give him "the look," then Nick said, "Yes, after that things changed, I changed."

118

"How?" Cuthbert asked.

"I didn't notice so much in the beginning. I cared but I didn't, does that make sense?" Nick said.

"I think so," Cuthbert said, "what were you doing differently?"

"I stopped viewing the cases I worked on as people. They were files, challenges to be solved," Nick said.

"You have done some good work, though," Cuthbert said, "provided closure for so many."

"No, Cuthbert, I didn't. I solved cases, but there is no closure for the loss of love ones," Nick said. "There was no real connection, it was a puzzle I solved and moved on."

"So, how was it different before, really?" Cuthbert asked.

"Well, there was a time when I involved myself instead of just observing," Nick said.

"How was that different?" Cuthbert asked.

"I don't know. I guess when the person I was dealing with opened up and I guess I opened up too, sounds silly," Nick said.

"It doesn't," Cuthbert said. "In fact, I think that's where I went wrong. I came in like gangbusters to fix you, Nick. I should have shared some of my life with you, but it was so long ago, and it was painful. I still don't like to think about it. I was on a similar path, not the same kind of path but a path where I was so consumed by my own shortcomings that I didn't appreciate what I had in my life and took the coward's way out until the very end."

"What happened at the very end?" Nick asked.

"My shortcoming was pride. I wasn't recognized as the artist I believed I was, so I began a long spiral down," Cuthbert said. "I turned my back on my wife, Lydia, and my daughter, Grace. I decided to give up and numb myself to my failure as an artist and a husband and a father. I embraced my guilt knowing that no one cared."

"So, you committed suicide by Four Roses?" Nick asked.

"I tried," Cuthbert said. "Believe me, but I was wrong; there was someone who cared. He couldn't stop the inevitable. He tried to save me several times, but I was determined, and I succeeded. I died as he held me waiting for help to come."

"Who was he?" Nick asked.

Cuthbert smiled. "You are a very good detective; some say you are one of the best in the country."

"Thank you," Nick said.

Cuthbert said, "We should open up and be honest with each other."

"I agree," Nick said.

"I'll start," Cuthbert said. "Nick, as I said, you are a great detective, so I know that you know who tried to save me, don't you, Nick."

"Yes, I do," Nick said. "It was my grandfather, Andrew Caldwell."

"He was a fine man. It's one of the reasons I was assigned to you and the reason I wanted to come here," Cuthbert said. "My God, this is turning into a Hallmark Christmas movie."

"You don't know the half of it," Nick said.

"What does that mean?" Cuthbert asked.

"You wanted me to open up, right?" Nick asked.

"Yes," Cuthbert said.

"In one of our awkward confrontations, you asked me, what I wanted," Nick said. "I'm going to ask you that as you look back at the life you have lived, what would you want?"

Cuthbert looked sad. "I would want to know that my family was all right, that even though I failed them they were able to overcome my failure and were happy and safe. I just would want to know that they were well cared for and..."

Nick said, "That's all I want to know. I want to know that my children, wherever they are, are well and cared for and loved."

"Nick, they are," Cuthbert said.

"Cuthbert, I want to know for sure," Nick said.

"Nick, you were right, neither Bob nor I have that kind of, as you put it, that kind of push, no one does. Nick, *'blessed are they that have not seen, and yet have believed.'*"

"You asked me what I want, what could put me back on a righteous path. That's it, I want a miracle," Nick said, with tears in his eyes. "I would do that for you."

"Nick, it's impossible and you know that," Cuthbert said.

"I know, but it's what I need," Nick said.

Nick stood, "Good night, Cuthbert, see you in the morning."

"Nick..." Cuthbert was interrupted.

"I understand, it's all right," Nick said.

The house was quiet, only Cuthbert sat in the living room alone, he looked up toward the ceiling and beyond to heaven and said, "Uriel can we talk?"

Chapter 32

The next morning, Nick left for the office with the pups before Bob or Cuthbert were stirring. Nick thought it was odd that they had to sleep at all.

He arrived at the office on a mission. He had come to terms that what he wanted most was impossible even for an angel. "Wait a minute," Nick said to Baron and Ruby, "I was able to say angel."

"I'll alert the media," Ruby said.

"Hey, you stole that from that old film *Arthur*; it was John Gielgud's line," Baron said, "movie reference."

"You two have been spending way too much time around Cuthbert," Nick said. "He isn't exactly a Clarence Odbody."

"Movie reference," Baron said.

"Who played Clarence?" Ruby asked. "Movie quiz."

"John Travers," Baron answered.

"Potter?" Ruby said.

"Barrymore," Baron snapped.

"John, Lionel or Drew," Ruby countered.

"Really?" Baron said. "Lionel."

"Ma Bailey?" Ruby said.

"Beulah Bondi," Baron said.

"Uncle Billy?" Ruby asked.

"Enough," Nick said.

Baron barked out, "Thomas Mitchell."

"I have to get to work," Nick said.

"Work," Baron said.

"*Work It*, a 2020 dance film, directed by Laura Terruso and written by Allison Peck," Ruby said.

"New movie reference," Baron barked.

"Are you done?" Nick said.

"You started it," Ruby said.

"Can I have a little quiet, please?" Nick asked.

"Quiet?" Baron thought. "All Quiet on the Western…"

"Baron." Nick said.

"Okay, okay, you should learn to chillax a little," Baron said, then hopped on the couch to pout.

Nick had Mike Butler's Quigle family tree in front of him. He went immediately through the list. He saw Lydia, Cuthbert's wife, then Emily his daughter, then Sarah, his granddaughter, then Maeve, his great granddaughter and finally, Maeve's daughter, Bridget five years old. Nick smiled.

He entered Maeve Burns and began to search and printed the information.

Maeve Burns was an artist, residing in Chicago. She had a loft on the Northside that was her gallery and workspace. She was listed as single with a daughter. She was a mystery and very private.

Nick looked up the number of the gallery. He just hadn't figured out what to say. He didn't think opening with *"Hey, Ms. Burns, how would you like to meet your dead great grandfather, who was an artist too and I think it would be really keen to bring your daughter to a mall to meet him since he was playing Santa there this Christmas, cool huh? Oh, by the way he's a Christmas Angel now."*

Nick decided to do what he always did in situations like this: he decided to be as vague as possible and be as truthful as possible.

He punched in the number. It rang three times and he decided to hang up, when he heard a voice, "Hello, the Burns Gallery."

"Hello, may I speak to Maeve Burns, if she is available?" Nick asked.

"Depends," the woman said.

Nick was taken aback. "Depends?"

"Sure," the woman said.

"I don't understand," Nick said.

"It depends what you want Maeve to be available for," the woman said.

"I need to talk with her about a personal matter," Nick said.

"May I say who's calling?" the woman asked.

Nick paused, "Oh, I'm sorry, my name is Nick Caldwell."

"Chicago's Sherlock Holmes, Nick Caldwell?" the woman asked.

Nick began to blush. "I'm just an investigator, that's all."

"You mean all those books are fiction," she asked.

"Let's say heavily embellished and very embarrassing," Nick said.

"You mean you're not the dashing and brave crime fighter in the books?" she asked.

"We do what we can," Nick said.

"Do you really have dogs that talk to you all the time?" she asked.

"Doesn't everyone?" Nick said.

"Of course," she replied.

"Well, could I leave my number and when Ms. Burns has some time would you ask her if she would call me?"

"I have a better idea, if it is a personal matter why don't you drop by the gallery later and speak with her in person?" she asked.

"I could do that," Nick said. "Oh, what's your name?"

"My name?" she asked.

"Yes, your name," Nick said.

"It's Maeve. I look forward to meeting you Nick, bye."

Chapter 33

Bob was sitting in the living room watching *A Charlie Brown Christmas* when Cuthbert came downstairs.

"Sleeping in, today?" Bob asked.

"I was up late talking to Nick," Cuthbert said.

"How'd it go?" Bob asked.

"Better until we 'opened up and were honest' and he told me what he wanted," Cuthbert said.

"He wants to see his children and know they are okay," Bob said.

"Yep," Cuthbert said.

"You explained that is impossible, right?" Bob said.

"Yeah," Cuthbert said.

"What happened?" Bob asked.

"We sat in silence for a while and then he went up to bed," Cuthbert explained. "He wasn't happy."

"You tried," Bob said.

"Well, I asked for guidance and contacted Uriel," Cuthbert said.

"What? You contacted Uriel? What were you thinking?" Bob said.

"I was thinking maybe I could find a loophole," Cuthbert said.

"A loophole?" Bob asked.

Cuthbert said, "Yeah, an exception, a..."

"I know what a loophole is, and I know there are no loopholes for this kind of thing," Bob said.

"That's what Uriel said, but he said he would check," Cuthbert said.

"He would check. Who was he going to check with?" Bob asked. "No, he's not going to check with..."

"Who do you think?" Cuthbert asked.

Bob almost gasped. "Not with 'J'? Oh Cuthbert."

"Uriel contacted me early this morning," Cuthbert said.

"What did he say?" Bob asked.

"He said that he was told that it would be impossible for an angel to arrange something like that and it would be improper for saints or administration to do something like that, but he thought there was someone who could arrange it for just a minute. He was told there was a loophole, but he had to get the spirit that might be able to help and see if he would," Cuthbert said.

"That's good, right?" Bob said.

"Not really, this spirit may not be willing to do it," Cuthbert said.

"Why?" Bob asked.

"Well, the spirit could do it but might not want to do it for me," Cuthbert said.

Chapter 34

As Nick drove to the Burns' Gallery, he thought about the somewhat strange conversation he had had with Maeve Burns. He could only remember having that kind of conversation with one other person.

He was stopped at a light and got a weird feeling in the pit of his stomach. He thought Maeve Burns…M.B. M… but if it were…no, the initial of the last name should be R not B. "I'm being silly, it couldn't be her, besides where would she have gotten a kid and how could she take on the identity of…," the blast of a horn behind him re-refocused Nick. "No, I'm being ridiculous, it can't be her."

He found a place to park in front of the gallery. It was on the second floor above a coffee shop. Nick entered and walked up the front steps. He was surprised that the building reminded him of his own building on Clark, with his offices above Blackies, now the Half Sour.

He opened the door and entered a small lobby with framed posters of the Burns Gallery opening, now also decorated for the Christmas season.

Nick noticed something that shocked him. On one wall there was a large portrait with a familiar looking face: it was Cuthbert. Nick smiled and thought Cuth needed to see this, so he took a picture of it. There was a plaque where it was written, *Cuthbert Quigle, noted Chicago artist who died before his time and the fountain of inspiration for a distant granddaughter. I will always honor and remember him and the one friend who helped him. Maeve Burns.*

Nick was taking a picture of the plaque when he heard a voice behind him.

"Are all Caldwells devotees of the memory of Cuthbert Quigle?"

Nick turned quickly and saw a woman standing with her arms folded. She was tall with long raven hair with flecks of grey strands. She looked like she was in her late twenties or early thirties, but Nick knew she was in her very early forties. Her face had all the good features that Cuthbert possessed, the penetrating eyes and smile. And after their first conversation, he suspected she had a similar personality...she was probably a smart ass.

"Not all Caldwells but I found out recently just the cops," Nick said.

"You were a cop, weren't you?"

"For a while but I strayed and was not let in on the tradition," he said.

"In my family, your grandfather was considered a saint and hero," she said.

To me, he was a man who told great stories, smoked a pipe, and always had peppermint sticks. He was a cops' cop. At least that's what my dad said," Nick replied.

"How is Billy? What a sweet man," Maeve said.

"You know my dad?" Nick said, surprised.

"Since I was a little girl, and he has never missed one of my openings," she said.

"I didn't know," Nick said.

"You're called the embodiment of Sherlock Holmes and you didn't know?" she laughed.

Nick thought, yes, this woman is definitely a relation of Cuthbert.

"I just do a job and try to help where I can," Nick said.

"You could have said, "aw-shucks ma'am," she said.

This time Nick laughed.

"I guess that did sound a bit like a *High Noon* Gary Cooper-ish," Nick said.

"Movie reference, not bad," she said.

"Nick laughed again. He thought she's definitely related to Cuthbert. "I watch a lot of movies," he said.

"Billy says that your office looks like, and I am quoting, 'a damn movie set from Maltese Falcon of Sam Spade's office,' with a Hall of Fame of movie detectives," she laughed.

"Sounds like him," Nick said, laughing.

"So, Sam, what are you here to talk about?" she asked.

"Well, I have a client who is an art lover of early Chicago artists and wants to write a book about artists in the twenties," Nick said.

"Really," she said, with a hint of skepticism.

"I have been tasked with finding decedents of those artists," Nick lied.

"Do a lot of this kind of work, do you, Sam?" Maeve asked. "I thought you did more cold cases, murders, serial killers, who dun-it kind of work, clearing people's names, you know PI stuff," she said.

"I handle a variety of cases and I like history," Nick stumbled.

"So, you are here to talk about Cuthbert?" she asked. "You could have asked your dad. He knows probably much more than I do."

"Through my investigation we have found that Cuthbert Quigle had five brothers that left Chicago in the early part of the century and spread out across the country," Nick lied and thought he was getting good at this. Maybe I should go into politics.

"I wouldn't know. I never heard anyone in my family ever mention that Cuthbert had family," she said. "This is interesting,"

"Yes, it is," Nick said. "I have found where his brothers moved to."

"Really?" she said.

"And I have found one of their decedents and he is in Chicago," Nick said. "He is a retired college professor and he decided to travel. He's doing this 'work-his-way-around-the-country kind of thing,' you know, get-out-of-the-ivory-tower thing, see-the-world-kind-of..."

"Thing?" she said.

"Yeah, that kind of thing," Nick said.

"Are you more articulate about crimes that involve mayhem and murder?" she asked, smiling.

"Nick looked at her and said, "Much."

"Do I get a chance to meet this long lost relative?" she asked.

"That's what I really came here to ask. I've grown fond of this guy while I was interviewing him. He doesn't really talk about the family and I get the sense that he is also the last of his line. I think he would like to meet you," Nick said.

"Okay, when and where?" Maeve said.

"Well, you also may want to bring your daughter," Nick said.

"Bridget, why?" she asked.

"We're going to the mall to meet him," Nick said.

"He works at the mall?" Maeve asked.

"I told you he was working his way across country," Nick said. "Well, he does it by taking seasonal or temp jobs."

"Okay, where does he work at the mall," Maeve asked, a little amused.

"He's Santa," Nick said.

"You mean I have a relative who is Santa Claus," Maeve said. She was delighted.

"Well, he plays Santa, he's not really..." Nick was interrupted.

"Anyone who plays Santa is Santa, the spirit of Christmas imprints them forever," Maeve said. "When do we leave?"

Nick said, "Well, I guess I could arrange it..."

"For now?" Maeve said, with the enthusiasm of a little girl.

"Don't you want to take your daughter?" Nick asked.

"She's in the studio. Bridget, Bridget..." she yelled.

A little girl appeared at the lobby door. She looked like a miniature version of her mother. "Bridge, we're going to go see Santa and guess what, he's related to us."

The little girl's eyes got bigger. "We're related to Santa Claus?" the little girl asked.

"We're related to this one," Maeve said.

130

"Momma, who is this gentleman?" Bridget asked.

"This is a 'gumshoe,'" Maeve said, laughing.

"Are you the real Sam Spade?" she asked. "Is your name Spencer? Because you don't look like a Hieronymus."

Nick laughed. "No, I'm not a Hieronymus, I'm Nick Caldwell."

"And you're a real detective?" she asked.

"It depends who you talk to," Nick said.

"Mom, is he a real detective?" Bridget asked.

"He is, Bridget," Maeve said.

"Is he a great detective?" she asked her mom.

Maeve smiled. "He could be if he learned to chillax."

"Mom, you think everyone should chillax," Bridget said.

"She's probably right," Nick said.

"What do you mean, probably," Maeve said, with a laugh. "So, let's go. Let me grab my sketch book."

Chapter 35

When Nick, Maeve and Bridget came through the mall's doors Bridget took off in a run towards the Santa Village. When Maeve and Nick arrived, Bridget was already in line to see Santa. Maeve couldn't take her eyes off Santa.

"His beard is real and it's white," she said.

"Santa usually has a white beard," Nick said.

"No, that's not what I mean. He is the very image of the picture in my gallery," she said.

"He is and that is because he is your long lost relative," Nick said.

She looked at him, "What's his name?" she asked.

"His name?" Nick said.

"You know, what someone may call another person," Maeve said.

"People call me a lot of different things," Nick said.

"I have no doubt," Maeve said with a grin, "but what is his name," pointing to Santa.

"Oh, his name, his name is Cuthbert Quigle, hot chocolate?" and Nick headed toward the Food Court.

"Wait a minute, Sammy," Maeve said. "It must have taken a lot of detective work to make the connection between my great grandfather and this Cuthbert."

"I am the Sherlock Holmes of Chicago," Nick said, with a dumb smile on his face.

"How did you find him?" she asked.

"I didn't. He found me, "Nick said, truthfully. "He was one of my professors in grad school at Michigan," Nick lied convincingly.

"Graduate School at Michigan," Maeve said.

"Yeah, GO BLUE." He lifted his right hand and punched the air.

Maeve looked at him.

"Maybe we should go meet Cuthbert," Nick said.

"Good idea," she said.

"You know I get the impression that you can be a very suspicious person," Nick said, joking.

"No, I'd be suspicious if you told me that Santa was the ghost of my great grandfather and believed it," Maeve said.

"What?" an alarmed Nick said. "No, I would never say something like that. I assure you he is not a ghost."

"Sam, chill, I'm kidding," Maeve said. "I know you don't talk to spirits. That's your business partner, right?"

"Sort of," Nick said and gave a nervous cheesy smile.

They walked up to Santa Village and Bridget was first in line. When it was her time, she hopped up next to Santa's chair and sat on the bench beside it.

Santa gave a grand "Ho, Ho, Ho," and said, "What's your name little one so I can look it up in my Naughty 'n Nice book."

Bridget boldly said, "Bridget Quigle Burns and I love you Santa."

Nick could see Santa was taken aback.

Santa asked, "Bridget Quigle Burns?"

"Yes, Santa," Bridget said proudly. "That's my Mom," and she pointed to Maeve. Her name is Maeve Quigle Burns. She's an artist like my great grandfather was. We have a picture of him in our gallery."

Cuthbert looked at Nick and Nick smiled. Cuthbert had a look of joy, accompanied with a few tears.

"What is your Christmas wish, Bridget Quigle Burns?" Santa said.

"I have to whisper it. I don't want anyone to know or it won't come true. You know that, Santa," Bridget said.

"Indeed, I do. I'm ready for you to whisper your wish," Santa said.

Bridget stood on the bench and whispered her wish.

Santa smiled. "That's an excellent wish; why don't we take a picture."

The mall photographer took several of Santa and Bridget.

Cuthbert looked at Maeve and said, "Would you honor me by taking a picture with me and your daughter?"

Nick thought he saw a tear in Maeve's eye. "I would be honored, Santa," Maeve replied.

Again, several pictures were taken.

Then Bridget said, "Santa could we have Mr. Caldwell in a picture with all of us? He is the one who brought me to see you."

"I think that's a wonderful idea," Santa said.

"Yeah, get up here, Sammy," Maeve said.

So, the picture was taken.

Santa's shift ended. Maeve and Cuthbert sat in the food court for hours talking, and Nick took Bridget to window shop.

Around four, Bridget said that she was getting hungry and Nick suggested that he call Bob and they all have an early dinner at Italian Village. Bridget was delighted, "May I have spaghetti?"

"Absolutely, if it's okay with your mom," Nick said.

Maeve nodded.

The dinner was very nice for Cuthbert, it was a family dinner, he beamed all evening. Cuthbert explained that Bob was a classmate of Nick's at Michigan. Cuthbert lied. He said that now he was a colleague at Michigan.

Bob responded with a less hearty, "Go Blue."

When the dinner was over, Nick dropped Maeve and Bridget back at the gallery and drove Cuthbert and Bob back to his house.

On the way back Bob said, "You did a good thing, Nick."

"The other night, I found out Cuthbert wanted the same thing I wanted, just to know his family was okay," Nick said. " I accepted that couldn't happen for me, so maybe the next best thing was to make it happen for someone else."

"Nick, I can never tell you how much I appreciate what you have done for me," Cuthbert said.

"Cuthbert, I was happy to do it," Nick said.

"You know, Cuthbert, Maeve is a beautiful woman and Bridget is angelic," Bob said.

"Absolutely," Cuthbert said, "she is beautiful, a talented artist, and has an enchanting spirit. She would be the perfect woman for the right..."

Nick interrupted Cuthbert and said, "Both of you stop it now or I'm going to lock the liquor cabinet."

"Like that would stop us," Bob said.

"Oh, Bobby, that was naughty," Cuthbert said and laughed.

They both began singing the *"Christmas Song"* replacing the lyrics *"Chestnuts roasting on an open fire"* with *"Chipmunks roasting on an open fire."*

As Nick drove, he mumbled, "You two would never get into a choir of A...un..g..., screw it."

There was hushed giggling coming from the back seat.

Chapter 36

Over the next week Maeve and Cuthbert spent a lot of time together. As it turned out, Nick's cover story was pretty accurate. He did in fact have brothers who left Chicago near the end of the second decade of the twentieth century. He never heard from any of them again.

Cuthbert was estranged from his family because who wanted a son or brother that was an artist, or writer or actor for that matter. These were not considered 'manly professions' on Cuthbert's side of the family. These were the professions of lazy men, drunkards and those who didn't want to get their hands dirty.

Nick was happy for Cuthbert, and Maeve was grateful to Nick for bringing them together. Cuthbert even convinced Nick to show Maeve and Bridget his real gumshoe's office. When Maeve saw the office she remarked, "Billy's right, it does look like a damn movie set."

When Cuthbert took her to lunch at the Half Sour, Nick stayed in the office with Bridget. She wanted to stay in the office. Nick suspected it wasn't so much because he was a real-life gumshoe but because she had made two new friends, Baron and Ruby. She would ask Nick every time she saw him if they were real life police dogs. Nick would say ask them and she did. She said they told her they were never police dogs but detective dogs. She was so matter of fact, he wondered if they really did talk to her. She was also a hit with Katie and Alana. She told them that when she grew up, she wanted to be a detective like them.

It was a couple of days before Christmas and Nick wondered how Maeve and Bridget would handle Cuthbert's unexplained departure. He also was a little sad that he probably wouldn't see them much after Cuthbert left, if at all.

That night the Burns women joined Cuthbert and Bob at Nick's house for a spaghetti dinner that Nick made especially for Bridget.

After dinner they sat in the living room and watched Christmas movies. As it got late, Bridget began to fade.

"I think it's time to go home, Bridge," Maeve said.

"I don't want to, Mommy. I want to do a sleep over with Baron and Ruby," she said.

Cuthbert immediately chimed in, "That's a wonderful idea."

"We couldn't, really," Maeve replied.

"Why not," Cuthbert said. "Nick has a pullout in his office. I would be happy to sleep there and you could have one of the guest rooms, right, Nick?"

"It's fine with me," Nick said. "I can run you guys home after breakfast in the morning."

"Please, Mom," Bridget said as Baron and Ruby wagged their tails.

Maeve looked at Nick, "Are you sure it wouldn't be any trouble?" she asked.

"Not at all," Nick said. "I even have extra toothbrushes that have never been used."

Maeve laughed. "Well, in that case, we accept."

Cuthbert said, "Wonderful, then it's settled. Nick will even make you pancakes in the morning."

"What kind?" Bridget asked.

"How about chocolate chip," Nick said.

"My favorite," the little girl said.

"Well, then off to bed," Maeve said.

Nick showed them to their room, and they were followed by Ruby and Baron.

Cuthbert said, "Perfect."

"Cuthbert, I know what you're thinking, and I don't think you should be meddling," Bob said.

"I'm not meddling. I am simply revealing possibilities," Cuthbert said.

Nick came back down and sat on the couch and a few minutes later Maeve joined them, and she sat next to Nick. Cuthbert looked at Bob and grinned.

"Is it going to be sad for you to play Santa for last time this year tomorrow," Maeve asked.

"A little but there is always next year," Cuthbert said. "It will be sad Christmas Day because Bob and I have to go on our way."

"Do you know where you are going next?" she asked.

"I think we will be going to Europe, right, Bob?" Cuthbert lied.

"Oh, yes, Europe," Bob lied.

"Where?" she asked.

"We haven't decided,' Bob said.

"What do you have to do tomorrow?" Cuthbert asked.

"After I drop Maeve and Bridget home, I'll go into the office for a while until I go on shuttle duty," Nick said.

"Shuttle duty?" Maeve asked.

"Yeah, my younger brother Phil and I are doing train station and airport pick up," Nick said. "We have to pick up my sister and brother-in-law and their twins at the train station and make an airport run to pick up Dalton Tate, Billy's former partner, and Sinclair Stewart. "I think you'll like Sinclair, he's a smart ass, too," Nick said.

"What do you mean too?" Maeve asked.

"You know exactly what I mean," Nick said, while Maeve laughed. "After that I guess I will come back here until the party. You know you and Bridget are invited."

"I did. Billy called me a couple of days ago," she said.

"Are you going to wear an ugly Christmas sweater?" she laughed.

"Probably not," Nick said.

"May I ask you a personal question?" she asked.

"Would it matter if I said no?" Nick asked.

"Of course not" she said, smiling.

"That's what I figured," Nick said.

"Do you own any clothing that is not navy blue, grey or black?" she asked.

Cuthbert and Bob laughed.

138

"I do, I have a Black Watch and a Stewart Plaid blazer," Nick said, proudly.

"Plaid?" she said.

"Plaid," he responded. "Why do you ask?"

"Just curious," she said. "I bet you have your closet organized by suit color and your shirts by color and stripes."

"Maybe," Nick said

"Oh, look at the time," Cuthbert said, "I have to get up early."

"Me too," Bob said.

"See you both in the morning," Cuthbert said.

Nick and Maeve were left on the couch.

"You know what they're doing, right?" Nick said.

"What are they doing?" she asked.

"They are trying to be matchmakers," Nick said.

"Really?" Maeve said, sarcastically. "I hope not. I like you, Nick, but you are far too old for my daughter. You're a mensch Caldwell."

"You're a bean láidir Burns."

"What does that mean?" she asked.

"It means you're a strong woman," Nick said.

"And we're both daoine duilich," she said.

What's that mean?" he asked.

"It's Gaelic for difficult people," she said.

They clinked their glasses and laughed.

Chapter 37

The phone rang early Christmas Eve morning. Nick was alone in the kitchen prepping for breakfast when he answered.

"Merry Christmas, Bro," Phil said.

"Yeah, Okay, what's up?" Nick asked.

"Hey, where's that Ho, Ho, Ho spirit; after all, you have St. Nick staying at your house," Phil said.

"Is there something you want?" Nick asked.

"Yeah, could I do the train station run and you take the airport?" Phil asked. "I have some Christmas shopping to finish."

"Sure, anything else?" Nick asked.

"Would you like to know my Christmas wish?"

"No," Nick said.

"My wish is that both my big brothers will find it in their hearts to pull those extremely large sticks out of their asses." Phil broke out laughing.

"You're pretty festive for a guy who says that he has the same psych scores as Gacy and Dahmer," Nick said.

In a very serious voice Phil said, "Maybe you and Wil should remember that."

"You should remember that we have stockpiled lots of dye, so for the New Year do you prefer pink, day-glow green, or the ever-popular yellow Haines briefs?" Nick said.

"You're an evil man, Nick Caldwell," Phil said.

"I know, but you oh brother are a looney toon."

"I'm rubber and you're glue; whatever, you say bounces off me and sticks to you," Phil said.

"I thought you were going to go with sticks and stones, again."

"Nope, you gotta mix it up," he said. "I'll talk to you later."

Maeve walked into the kitchen with her wet hair in a towel and Nick's robe on.

Nick looked at her.

"Hey, big boy, you like what you see?" she said.

'Yeah, terrycloth really gets my blood going," he said.

"Let's try that again,: she said. "Hey, big boy, like what you see?"

"Compared to what?" Nick said with a laugh.

"You do realize, Sammy, I will not forget, and I will get you for that."

"Good thing I carry a gun," Nick said.

"Yeah, but haven't you been on the receiving end of the whole gun play thing in recent years?" she said.

"I use it to give my adversaries a false sense of security," Nick said.

"Why, so they can try to finish you off in your hospital room where you can overpower them with a bed pan?" she said.

"Finally, someone gets my strategy," Nick said.

Bridget strolled in with Baron and Ruby close behind.

"Are we still having pancakes?" Bridget asked.

"We are," Nick said. "How do you like them?"

"On a plate with syrup," she answered.

"You are your mother's daughter," Nick said.

Cuthbert rumbled down the stairs. "I have to get to work; last day can't be late."

"You want some breakfast?" Nick asked.

"Of course I want breakfast, but I don't have time," Cuthbert said, "not necessary. You stay here with the lovely Maeve and the enchanting Bridget."

Cuthbert headed to the door and then turned. "Nick, can I speak to you for a moment?"

"Sure," Nick said. They went into the living room.

"Nick, the mall closes at four today," Cuthbert said, "do think we could talk for a little while before the party this evening?"

"I should be back here by four, we can talk then," Nick said.

"Fine. Maeve is wonderful, isn't she?" Cuthbert said.

"She is very nice," Nick said.

"And Bridget, what a beautiful child," Cuthbert said.

"She is," Nick said.

Cuthbert smiled. "You know, Nick…"

"Don't you need to get to work?" Nick said.

"You are correct, we will talk later." Cuthbert said and made a grand exit.

Nick walked back into the kitchen. "Do you like the pancakes, Bridget?"

"I do, but I'm sad that you didn't make any pancakes for Baron and Ruby," she said. 'They said they would like some pancakes too."

"They told you that they wanted pancakes?" Nick asked.

"Yes," she said.

"They talked to you?" Nick asked.

"Yes, they did, don't they talk to you?" Bridget asked

"That's an interesting question," Nick said.

"Baron told me there was something special about jazz and Chicago late at night when it rains," she said.

Nick looked at Baron and Ruby. If dogs could smile, they did.

Nick looked at Bob who had come into the kitchen while he was talking to Cuthbert. He walked up to Nick and whispered, "They did, and she heard them. I know it's eight in the morning, but can I get you a drink?"

Nick looked at Bob.

Maeve asked, "What are you two up to?"

In unison, they looked at her said, "Nothing."

Nick said, "Would you like coffee or a drink?"

"A drink at eight o'clock in the morning, are you nuts?" Maeve said laughing.

"I think the answer to that question is obvious," Nick said.

Chapter 38

Nick spent the day at the office looking over potential cold cases until he had to pick up Sinclair Stewart at the airport.

All morning as he went through the cases he would talk to Baron and Ruby, but all they answered was "woof." They weren't barking, they were saying "Woof." And then if dogs could giggle...they were.

He headed for the airport to pick up Sinclair. Throughout the ride Baron and Ruby sat in the backseat giggling. Nick said to himself, "Now it's official, I have lost my mind."

Sinclair was waiting outside the terminal when Nick drove up.

He got in the car and said, "Have your house guests stolen your silverware yet?"

"They're okay," Nick said.

"They're okay?" Sinclair said. "I couldn't find any record of either one of those two jokers. I couldn't even find anything about them at the university."

"So, you're saying I didn't take classes from Cuthbert, or are you saying I'm a liar," Nick said.

"I'm saying I didn't find anything out that makes sense except that the name Cuthbert Quigle appears only in two public records, a birth certificate and a death certificate in 1927," Sinclair said.

" So, the most obvious logical conclusions are that the Cuthbert Quigle I know is either an alias, or that I took classes from a ghost, or he is figment of my imagination that is so severe it caused a mass hysteria with me, you, my staff, and my family?"

"No, I'm saying there is something fishy going on?" Sinclair said.

"Oh, there is another possibility: this Cuthbert that died in 1927 has come back to life and he brought a friend from the hereafter to show me the errors of my life so that I will change my ways and become a better person and save me from myself?" Nick said.

"You mean, like in *A Christmas Carol* or *It's a Wonderful Life*?" Sinclair said.

"Yeah," Nick said, "after all, it's the right season for that kind of thing."

"That would make those two weirdos angels. That's crazy. The one thing I am sure about is that those two are not angels." Sinclair let out a loud laugh.

"Are you sure?" Nick said, with a smile.

"If you think those two are angels, you are crazier than I think you are; no, you are crazier than anyone on the planet." Sinclair laughed again.

"Where do you want to go, a hotel?" Nick asked.

"I'm staying at Billy's and so is Dalton. After the party and all you young'uns go home to bed and start dreaming of sugar plums and Santa, your father, Dalton and I are going to do some serious card playing and drinking," Sinclair said.

Nick rolled up in front of Billy's house.

"Are the angels coming to the party tonight?" Sinclair asked.

"Pretty sure they are. Either they'll drive over with me and the pooches, or I guess they could fly over here," Nick said.

"You're an idiot sometimes, you know that," Sinclair said.

"Tell me something I haven't heard before," Nick said. "See you later." As promised, Nick drove home for his talk with the A...un...gel...s screw it."

Chapter 39

Cuthbert was on the couch when Nick arrived. "You're early," Nick said.

"Yes," Cuthbert said, "Santa's Village closed early so they could repair for the after Christmas sales...barbarians."

"I agree. What do you want to talk about?" Nick asked.

"Bob and I are departing tonight after evening Mass. I hope you will attend with us, sort of a spiritual farewell tradition," Cuthbert said.

"I thought you were sticking around until New Years?" Nick said.

"We were, but I am betting that you will be busy, possibly New Year's Eve." Cuthbert smiled.

"I don't know about that," Nick said.

"We do," Bob said as he entered the room.

"You two don't have to leave if you don't want to," Nick said.

"Nick, we don't need to be here any longer. What you did for Cuthbert, Maeve and Bridget proves you have opened your heart," Bob said.

"That was nothing, I knew I couldn't find out about my family that are gone, so I thought maybe I could give that to someone who wanted what I wanted," Nick said.

"You did, my friend. I wanted to know how my loved ones fared and you gave me that. Maeve wanted to feel closer to her heritage and you gave her that," Cuthbert said. "You did that."

"Nick, we want you to realize where you were and where you are now," Bob said. "You have accepted what has happened, but by no means do we expect you to move on. There will be a hole in your heart, a hole in your life forever, but we believe you can move forward with your life."

"I don't feel much different," Nick said.

Cuthbert looked at Baron. "Well."

"You're always good to us but you didn't even tell Sinclair to go...well you know," Baron said.

"Yeah, and you haven't dyed Phil's underwear pink or yellow," Ruby said.

"Yet," Nick said.

"I left you two gifts. After Mass tonight come home and one will be delivered to you. The second gift will be delivered in the morning. Promise me you will be here to receive them," Cuthbert said.

"Okay, I promise," Nick said.

"There are a couple of other things we need to talk to you about before we leave," Bob said. "You know that once we leave no one we have met here will remember we were here. That includes you, Nick."

"What about us?" Baron asked.

"Oh, you'll remember, but it's a good thing you can't talk," Cuthbert said, with a wink and laugh.

"Yeah, That's a good thing, right Ruby?"

"Absolutely," Ruby said with a doggie smile.

"Tonight, at the party we will make sure that all the good things that have come about will be remembered, but there will be no memory of our visit," Bob said.

"How are you going to that?" Nick asked.

"How do you think, we're...," Cuthbert said, and then he smiled at Nick, "go ahead Nick say it."

Nick looked at him and said hesitantly, "Because you're Angels."

"Now was that so hard?" Cuthbert said and roared with laughter.

Bob said, "Well, I'm going to go get ready for the party."

"So am I," Cuthbert said. "Nick, I have something for you. It's not what you hoped for, but it is something." He handed Nick a letter. "If you need to talk after you read it, I'll be upstairs."

Nick was left in the living room with Baron and Ruby and an ominous envelope.

He opened it and began to read:

Dear Nick,

Your friend came to me and asked if I could consider reuniting with the family.

I'm sorry, Nick, maybe if Mom was still around but she isn't. Our father and I had a falling out about who I am and whether I should run my life or whether he should run my life; I opted for me. I want you to know it wasn't easy for me to leave you and Wil. I am your big sister, and I was your first babysitter. If it makes you feel better, you were a good kid and Wil was a little shit; he reminded me a lot of Billy.

My leaving had nothing to do with Mom or you or Wil. Billy and I are just to alike and we never got along. I was never going to want to be a cop and he was never going to forgive me for not being wanting to be a cop. I'm sure in some small way you understand. Wil was always the great hope; he wanted to be a cop from the time he was a little kid.

You were different; even as a kid you wanted to help people. Nick, I almost contacted you after you lost Mary and I found out that Annie lost your other child. I tried and I apologize, I just couldn't. My only regrets are that I didn't meet your family and I never got to know Phil and Laura.

I have followed your career and your big sister is very proud of you. You have lived your life on your terms. Maybe one day we will meet. I hope so.

Nick, it wasn't easy to walk away from the family or the good memories I had with Mom, you and Wil and even some good memories of Billy, but sometimes you have to be on your own to recover.

I wish you the best and please stop getting shot.

Take care, brother,

Your absent Sister.

Nick put the letter down and looked at Baron and Ruby and said, "It must have been hard to just leave everything you knew and start a new life.

Baron said, "Yep."

"She must have been very hurt and very scared to do something like that," he said.

"Yeah, it must have been tough for Annie after she lost Mary and little Wil to go on. She probably had to get away from the memories, too," Baron said, and then he and Ruby walked out of the room.

Chapter 40

The Caldwell Christmas Party was Billy's favorite. He liked that his family and extended family gathered to celebrate the holiday. His children and grandchildren were there. So were his friends and the friends that he had in Nick's agency.

When Nick arrived, his brothers and sister and her family were already there. Wil's fiancé was also helping set up. Cuthbert greeted Billy who said, "Cuthbert, how are you? Cuthbert, that's a common name isn't it?"

"It is Billy, it is. It is great to see you again," Cuthbert said. "Billy, where is the whiskey?"

"In the kitchen," Billy said. "Find Sinclair and you'll find the whiskey."

"Wonderful," Cuthbert said. He walked into the kitchen and Sinclair who was there looked up.

"Well, if it isn't the elusive Mr. Quigle," Sinclair said.

"It is, and how are you, Mr. Stewart?" Cuthbert said.

"May I ask you a question?" Sinclair said.

"Certainly, it's Christmas, what do you wish to ask? Cuthbert replied.

"Okay," Sinclair said, "what exactly is your story? I can't find any record of who you are. What kind of con are you running here?"

"I'm not running a con, as you put it, but I will be happy to tell you my story and why I am here."

"I'm listening," Sinclair said.

"Good," Cuthbert said. "Well, I was an artist and a pretty bad drunk when I died in 1927. For some unexplained reason I was made a Christmas Angel and I was teamed with Bob. You know Bob, you met him at Thanksgiving, and I assume you believe he is a part of some 'con' too. Bob is Nick's Guardian Angel. This Christmas we have come back to earth. We have been charged with, well, kind of saving Nick from himself, you know to clean up his act, stop torturing people in basements and such."

"You know about that?" Sinclair said.

"Of course, and I also know that you were very troubled about that and you were very concerned about the direction of Nick's life," Cuthbert said. "You are a good man Mr. Stewart, and we know you tried to talk to Nick about that. It was one of your prayers that also helped us get assigned. So, we've made tremendous progress with him and he has changed for the better. I see a great future for him."

Sinclair looked at him for a moment and said, "You're an…"

"Yes, I'm an Angel," Cuthbert said, and he looked into Sinclair's eyes and said very slowly "and I know that you will always keep my little secret and you will never tell anyone and after tonight you won't even remember Bob and I were here or our mission, right?"

Sinclair looked at Cuthbert and said, "I will always keep my little secret and you will never tell anyone and after tonight you won't even remember Bob and I were here or our mission, right?"

"That's fantastic, because you are a good man, you will have a hunch when you get back to New Orleans, do you understand?" Cuthbert said.

"When I get home to New Orleans, I will have a hunch," Sinclair said.

"Do you will remember the name Fontane Barbeau?" Cuthbert asked.

"I think he was a dance teacher, yes, he was my daughter's dance teacher," Sinclair said.

"That's right,' Cuthbert said. "Mr. Barbeau is close to your age and not a very good person. You will open your daughter's case and you will tell the police that you got a tip that Mr. Barbeau has a little lock box hidden in the office of his studio. In that box they will find the locket you gave your daughter with her initials on it and inside the locket there is…"

"A picture of her mother and me," Sinclair said.

Cuthbert said, "There will also be other items of young girls that he has hurt. You then will bring him to justice. I'm sure Nick will help but remember you will not know where you got this information. This will be painful, but it will take away some of the pain you have been carrying. Merry Christmas, my friend.

Sinclair said, "Merry Christmas."

"Good, now let's get pissed," Cuthbert said.

As they toasted, Nick walked in. "What's going on here?"

"I'm having a drink with my friend Cuthbert here; he's got great stories," Sinclair said.

"I bet he does," Nick said.

"I'm going to go help Billy. We'll get back to drinking later, Cuth," Sinclair said and left the kitchen.

"Cuth, you guys are buds now?" Nick asked.

"And why not, we are men of the world," Cuthbert said. "Oh, by the way, if after the first of the year, Sinclair asks you to go to New Orleans, don't ask questions, just go, promise."

"Okay," Nick said, "but..."

Cuthbert smiled and said, "Just go."

"Oh, Maeve and Bridget have arrived," Nick said.

"Wunderbar!" Cuthbert said, "I'm going to Europe, you know."

+

Maeve and Bridget were talking with Billy, Bob, and Laura when Cuthbert and Nick walked up.

"Maeve, have you met my son Nick?" Billy said.

"I believe so, he looks very familiar," Maeve said.

"I like his pancakes," Bridget said

"Billy looked a little confused as he introduced Cuthbert to Bob and Laura, "This is Cuthbert Quigle and from what I just heard from Maeve, you two are distant relatives."

"Yes, we are," Cuthbert beamed.

Billy said, "Are you sure, there seem to be a lot of Cuthbert Quigles out there."

151

"Not as many as you think, Dad," Nick said.

"So, how are you doing tonight, Sammy," Maeve asked.

"Okay. I'm always a little sad at this party. We all look forward to it and then midway through, I realize it's almost over and we have a New Year in front of us," Nick said.

"Are you sure you're Scot-Irish and not Russian?" Maeve asked and laughed.

Nick laughed too. "I know, but it's been a long year for all of us."

Maeve said, "Come on, Nick, enjoy what's going on in your life. From what I understand, your business partner has become a business genius. You have the Investigation and Security office, the St. Louis office and the Clark street Office. You've done some good things. There's a series of books based on your 'adventures,'" she laughed, "and Cuthbert told me that you were going to start practicing law in the new year. He also said that you will probably get an offer from one of the universities to lecture."

Wil, Nick's older brother, said, "Lecture on what, how to get shot?"

Phil chimed in, "Maybe he could lecture on advance interrogation procedure."

Wil and Nick in unison said, "Shut up, Pinkie."

Maeve laughed and said to Phil, "Your brothers call you 'Pinkie'?"

"It's a long story," Phil said, "a story of cruelty by two older brothers on their impressionable little brother, it's really quite sad."

Laura said, "I don't know what Phil's talking about. Nick and Wil have always been great to me."

"That's because you're the youngest and the girl," Phil said, acting like he was pouting.

Laura said sarcastically, "You're so mature."

They all laughed.

"Maeve," Laura said, "I love your gallery. Bob and I went and looked at it the last time we were up here. I really like that you have a variety of different styles."

"Thank you. We usually try to give new artists a chance, particularly street artists," Maeve said.

"You know that Billy has one of your great grandfather's paintings in his office here," Laura said. "I grew up with that painting; he was amazing."

"I liked his work very much. There is more than you think out there," Maeve said. "The story goes that he burned a lot of his work around the time he died, but he still had work out there."

Bridget, who had been in an intense conversation with Baron, said, "Nick's a detective, we should ask him to find all those paintings."

Nick asked, "Why do you think I could find all those paintings?"

Bridget said, "Well, you found Cuthbert, my mom and me, and Baron said, you find all sorts of bad guys too."

"He did, huh?" Nick said.

"And he said you found him and Duke and Tina, and a lot of other dogs," she said.

Nick looked at Baron as he turned to see if anyone had dropped any food.

+

The party was still going strong at ten o'clock. Bridget had been thrilled to meet Bart and particularly his husband, Jonathan, when she found out he used to play for the Bears because she had a lot of teddy bears and one of them even had a football jersey. Jonathan and Bart listened to all her stories about her Bears. She spent most of the evening talking to Constance, Katie, and Alana about being a lady detective.

Maeve spent a lot of time huddled with Laura and Mrs. Marbulls; Nick knew this couldn't be good for him. Felix and Greg spent the evening talking about the latest criminal scientific procedures. Everyone seemed to have a good time, even Bob who was debating religious philosophy with two of Billy's friends who were retired Jesuits and seemed to be having fun.

Nick, around ten thirty began saying his goodbyes. He planned to drop Baron and Ruby at home before Mass. As Nick, Cuthbert and Bob were leaving, Maeve came up to them and hugged Cuthbert and Bob. It was an emotional goodbye.

When Cuthbert and Bob headed to the car with the pups, Maeve stopped Nick and said, "I can't thank you enough for making all this happen for Bridget and me."

"I really didn't do much, but I am happy that it meant something to you and Bridget," Nick said.

"You know, Nick, what you need to do?" Maeve said.

Nick smiled and said, "I have a feeling you are going to tell me. Oh, wait, I know this one, I need to Chillax."

"That too," she said, "but you need to give yourself a break; you're not a bad guy, you're one of the good guys. For Bridget and me you're an angel."

Nick laughed. "I am pretty sure I'm not an angel but thank you."

"I like you, Caldwell," she said.

"I like you too, Burns," he said.

"Good," she said.

"Good," he said.

"See you around," she said.

"Yeah, see you around," Nick replied.

"Okay," she said.

"Well, okay, then," Nick said.

"Merry Christmas," she said.

"Merry Christmas to you and Bridget," he said.

"Good night," Maeve said.

"Good night," Nick said.

Phil and Wil were standing on the porch watching this.

"Wil said to Phil, "You know, our brother is..."

"A moron?" Phil said.

Wil said, "I was going say idiot."

"That works too," Phil said.

"It's getting cold, let's go in, Pinkie," Will said.

"Would you please stop calling me that?" Phil asked.

Wil smiled. "Probably not."

"You know it's not funny," Phil said.

"It is to me and your idiot brother," Wil said.

Phil said, "You do know that my psych tests were in the same range as..."

Wil laughed "Yeah, yeah, yeah."

+

After Mass, Bob, Nick and Cuthbert stood in the church parking lot.

"I don't know what to say, I've gotten used to having you around," Nick said.

"You've done well," Bob said.

"I can say, I have enjoyed every minute, even the tense ones," Cuthbert said. "Remember what we talked about this afternoon."

"I will," Nick said, "I promise."

"I don't know how to thank you, Nick, for what you did for me," Cuthbert said.

"You don't have to," Nick said.

"You know, Nick, I am always with you," Bob said.

They stood there for a few moments.

"Well, I'm not going to say goodbye," Cuthbert said. "I will just say farewell."

There was a very tall young man with almost golden hair standing at the end of the parking lot.

Bob looked at him and said, "Time to go, there's our ride, take care of yourself, Nick."

"And, Nick, I just wanted to say, "Isn't Maeve a peach?"

Nick smiled "You better catch your ride."

"Oh," Cuthbert said, "say farewell to Baron and Ruby, you should listen to them more."

155

Bob and Cuthbert began walking toward the young man. When they got about twenty feet away from the young man, they disappeared into the night.

Chapter 41

Nick was exhausted when he got home after church. It was hard to tell if Baron and Ruby were tired because at this time of night they were usually sprawled out on the couch snoozing.

Nick went into the kitchen and made some hot chocolate; it's Christmas isn't it? Of course, being a detective and all, he also added some Bailey's. He sat between the pups clicking through the channels looking for something to watch. He had been boycotting *The Christmas Story* since they had started running it continually and since he decided that he wanted to be the one that shot little Ralphie's eye out.

He stopped clicking when he found "The *Bishop's Wife*, which was one of his favorite Christmas movies. It had a great whimsical story about an Episcopal Bishop that prayed for guidance and got an angel instead. It was made in 1947, directed by Henry Koster and written by Leonardo Bercovici and Robert E. Sherwood, with an amazing cast: Cary Grant Loretta Young, David Niven, Elsa Lanchester, Monty Woolley, James Gleason, Gladys Cooper, Karolyn Grimes and Regis Toomey.

Nick found himself, yelling "Movie reference," startling himself. "Where the hell did that come from?" he said to himself. Baron and Ruby looked at him, then laid their heads down.

Nick dozed off and as the story goes, when out on the lawn there arose such a clatter, Nick sprang from his couch holding his Glock 19 to see what was the matter. He looked out the window and there was nothing there. He turned around and was shocked to see standing by his fireplace a man, 6'2", about two-hundred and fifteen pounds, with a white beard, dressed in a red suit.

"You know, Nick, it would be naughty to plug me, particularly on Christmas."

"Put your hands up," Nick said.

Baron rolled his eyes; Ruby shook her head.

"Really?" Santa said.

"What are you doing here?" Nick said.

"I'm from the government to take your guns," Santa said.

"Really," Nick said.

Santa shook his head. "'No."

Nick lowered his gun.

"May I ask you a question?" Santa said. "Are you really one of the top detectives in Chicago?"

"I don't know, I just try to do my job," Nick said.

"But you are a good detective, right?" Santa said.

"I guess," Nick said.

"Well, do you think you could find me some cookies?" Santa said, with a laugh.

Ruby and Baron were laughing too.

Baron said, "Boy, that Santa's funny."

"He should do Vegas," Ruby said.

Nick asked, "Cookies? Would Scottish short bread be okay?"

"Even better," Santa said.

Nick went to the kitchen and brought out the tin and a glass of milk.

"I'll have to pass on the milk. I'm a little lactose intolerant," Santa said.

"Oh, sorry, I didn't know," Nick said.

"If you get the chance, pass the word will you. Most everywhere I go there's a glass of milk," Santa said.

"Is there something else I could get you?" Nick asked.

Santa smiled, "You wouldn't happen to have any Dewar's or Jamison's world you?"

"Both," Nick said.

"You are," Santa smiled, "a good boy. I think since I'm having shortbread, I'll trouble you for the Dewar's and pour one for yourself; in a few minutes you're going to need it."

"No trouble at all," Nick said, looking confused. "Why will I need it? Santa, why are you here?"

"Nick, I am here because I have to deliver to you a gift and it had to be delivered off the books," Santa said.

"A gift?" Nick said. "What kind a of gift?"

"A special gift, a gift after you receive it you will wonder if it was real," Santa said, "but in your heart you will know it was real and the hope is that it will give you hope, and it will ease your fear and pain. Now finish your drink and sit down."

Nick did as he was told.

Santa stood in front of the fireplace and put his arms out, slowly two small figures appeared, a little boy and a little girl. They smiled at Nick. The little boy waved, and the little girl blew Nick a kiss like she had every day when he had left for work. The little girl mouthed, "We love you Daddy," then they were gone.

Nick began to cry.

"That's okay, boy, let it out; you've been holding it in for far too long," Santa said. "Your Christmas wish has always been to know they were all right. Now you know they are, and you know they love you very much. It's time for you to move forward with your life."

Nick sobbed, "Will I ever see them again?"

Santa smiled, "Well, you didn't shoot Santa tonight and you gave me Dewar's and shortbread, so I'd say that's a good start."

Nick laughed a little. "Thank you."

"I'm just the messenger, you know who to thank. I have to go. Blessed Christmas, Nick."

"To you too, Santa," Nick said.

"Oh, I have one more message to deliver to you, from a friend you may not remember," Santa said.

"Who?" Nick asked.

"Doesn't matter," Santa said. "He said to ask you four questions." Santa began to check a list. "The first is, when you were a boy, who was your favorite comedian?"

"What?" Nick asked.

"You heard the question," Santa said.

"George Burns," Nick said.

"Who is the greatest Scottish writer," Santa asked.

"There are a lot of them, but I would say, Robert Burns," Nick said.

"Finally, in one of your favorite movies *The Usual Suspects*, who was your favorite character?' Santa asked.

"Keaton," Nick said, absolutely confused.

"Who played that character? Santa asked.

"Gabriel Byrne," Nick answered.

Santa checked his list again. "Now, I am supposed to say to you, 'GET IT?' And it says here, I must throw my head back, laugh loudly and say the following. So, here goes. 'Ho, Ho, Ho, Movie Reference! Ho, Ho, Ho."

"What?" Nick stood and said, but Santa was gone.

Nick, poured another drink and sat back on the couch in a state of, well, just in a state.

Ruby whispered to Baron, "Cuthbert."

Baron smiled. "You gotta love that guy."

Chapter 42

Nick was sprawled out of the couch, just ready to begin his Christmas morning hangover. There was a loud knocking on the front door. He yelled, "Go away."

The knocking continued. "Va Via," Nick said.

"Oscail an doras," a voice yelled back.

"What the…," Nick said. He slowly staggered to the door and opened it.

"I didn't know you spoke Italian," she said.

"Only when I'm hungover," Nick said.

"So, you're fluent," she said.

"You're a regular comedienne," Nick said, then paused for a moment and tried to think about something but couldn't remember what.

Do you always go to Christmas mass and then come home and get sloshed?" Maeve asked.

"Yes, are you writing a book?" Nick said, as he walked away from the door. "And what are you doing here so early in the morning?"

"Early," she said, "it's almost ten thirty."

"That's early, if you have a hangover," Nick said.

"What's wrong with you?" she asked.

"Nothing… I think I pulled a gun on Santa Claus last night," he said.

"That will get you on the naughty list,' she said. "Did you shoot him?"

"No, don't be silly," Nick said.

"Did he shoot you?" Maeve asked.

"No, Santa doesn't shoot people," he said, sitting back on the couch.

"That must have been a pleasant change for you, "she said.

"Is that supposed to be funny?" he asked.

"Extremely," she said.

"Have you told me why you are here at this early hour yet?" he said.

She said, "Up Dog."

"Up Dog? What's Up Dog?"

"Nothin,' What's up with you, Dog," she said, and broke into almost uncontrollable laughter, which led Nick to start laughing.

"Are you crazy?" Nick said, laughing.

"I'm here aren't I?" she said.

"Yes, you are," Nick said. "But the question remains, why?"

"Well, I was invited last night to go to Christmas brunch by your father. I arrived at your dad's house at ten. He said that he had been calling you since eight and you weren't answering. Bridget's hanging with Laura and the twins, and this is really weird, Wil was doing wash at your dad's."

Nick smiled and asked, "Where was Phil?"

"He was running an errand for Wil," she said.

Nick smiled again.

"So, Wil and your dad asked me to come over and see that you got there," she said.

"He did, did he, and of course my dad was all for it?" Nick said.

"He was; he even invited Bridget and me to attend New Year's Eve open house. He said it was the most important Scottish holiday of the year and at midnight everyone sang *Auld Lang Syne* by candlelight."

"That's weird," Nick said.

"He said you all did that every year," Maeve said,

"Yeah, we do?" Nick said.

"He said that it would be fun, and all the usual suspects would be there: Bob, Laura, Wil and Phil and the folks from your office, and many of them would be kilted," Maeve said. "He thought it would be interesting for me."

He said that?" Nick said.

162

"He did," she said, "what's wrong, you don't want me to go?"

"No, I do, it would be great, but, excuse me, do you think I have time for a drink?" Nick asked.

"No, you have time to take a shower and get dressed while I confer with Baron and Ruby. When you come down, if you are nice," Maeve said, "I will give you your Christmas present."

"I didn't get you anything," Nick said.

"You sure did, because of your investigation, I learned more about my family than I ever knew. It was sweet of you to give me all those files," she said.

"All those files?" Nick asked.

"Yes, they were gift wrapped under your father's Christmas tree. Why didn't you give them to me last night?" Maeve asked.

"Oh, aum, we always open our presents on Christmas day," Nick said

"Nice save," Baron said to Ruby.

"Yep, he pulled that one out," she said.

"I think I'll go get ready." Nick said.

A half hour later, he came back down showered and pressed.

"Okay, we ready?" he asked.

"We are, but first I wanted to give you your present," she said.

She handed him two flat packages.

"Thank you but it..." Nick said.

"Shut up, gumshoe, and open them," Maeve said.

He opened the first one and it was a framed sketch of her great grandfather Cuthbert Quigle. It was beautiful and was different from the portrait at the gallery, the old boy was smiling. He opened the second and it was a sketch of the picture that was taken at the mall with the two of them and Bridget with Santa. Nick thought that she was really a very fine artist.

I really love that picture," she said.

"It's wonderful," Nick said.

"You know, that was the best Mall Santa I have ever seen," she said.

"Yeah, I think you're right," Nick said. "Okay pups, time to go to Billy's."

They hopped off of the couch and headed for the door.

As they got in the car, Maeve said, "This has been a wonderful holiday."

"It has," Nick agreed. "I like you, Burns, despite your eccentricities."

"I like you, Caldwell, because of your contrariness," she said.

"I'm not contrary," Nick said.

"You are too," Maeve said.

"I'm not," Nick insisted. "Do you always have to have the last word?"

"Yes." Maeve laughed. "Now drive, we're already late."

He drove.

+

A guardian angel, a Christmas angel, a little girl and her brother walked into a coffee shop with nine dogs and sat down to have hot chocolate. When it arrived, they high fived each other, then they picked up their hot chocolate, and an older dog, named Duke, who was considered a hero in these parts, toasted, "To Nick."

The End

Biography

A Christmas Project is Wm. Sharpe's seventh novel and the fifth in the Nick Caldwell series. He developed a love for the detective mystery which he calls *"neo noir pulp."* As to why he calls it that, he has only said he "likes how it sounds." He did say "that mysteries, thrillers, suspense, and imaginary fiction are guilty pleasures to have fun with and to escape from day-to-day hum drum and the nightly news. They are written to be enjoyed." He suggests when reading them you hide your copy inside a cover of *War and Peace.* You will enjoy your read and make your friends believe that you are a serious intellectual.

He became interested writing paperback mysteries because his father loved them. He began writing because his mother wrote; unfortunately, she would never share her writing with the famlly. He explains that "Sometimes such is the way of Irish and Scottish families, 'controlled dysfunction,' we are born with a sense of sarcasm, humor and a wealth of stubbornness and crankiness."

Sharpe lives in Saint Louis, Missouri, with his wife Linda and Baron and Ruby, their ferocious BearhounDs. They enjoy visits from their son and daughter, Eric and Elise. Eric lives with his ferocious black cat Tinkerbell and Elise lives with her ferocious puppy Sheiky.

When not working on a story, he hunts for treasure in secondhand stores and he appears on two podcasts, UnCommonSense Radio 3.0 "the Podcast" with Lou Conrad and James Sodon, where his job is to be cranky. He also appears with James Sodon on "Novel Approach," a podcast about books and writing. He also watches anything that is streaming so he doesn't have to watch the news.

His day job is teaching, but most of the time now he spends staying indoors, washing his hands, trying to find the properly fitted mask and of course complaining loudly.

Books by Wm. Sharpe

Death by Lethal Affection
Justice Delayed
Uncle Joe is Dead
Not Forgotten
When Christmas Trees Flew
Dead Crowe
A Christmas Project

* * *

Made in the USA
Monee, IL
11 June 2023

35479796R00095